Soaring Betrayal

T. L. Cooper

The TLC Press

Soaring Betrayal

ISBN: 0984686282
ISBN-13: 978-0-9846862-8-5

The TLC Press
Albany, Oregon

All stories in this book are works of fiction. Names, characters, places, public or private institutions, corporations, town, and incidents are the product of the author's imagination or are used factiously. Any resemblance to actual events, locales, or persons, living or dead, is coincidental.

Dedication

Dedicated to anyone who has soared above betrayal to discover the strength within as well as to the people in my life whose betrayal pushed me to find my wings.

Contents

Acknowledgments

Once again Loay Abu-Husein took my vague description of what I wanted for the cover and turned it into something better than the image in my head. This collaboration took much back and forth to get it just right. I appreciate his tireless support, patience, efforts, and love more than he'll ever know.

I send my immense gratitude to Joanne Pence for her feedback on individual stories as well as on the cover! Her input was far more valuable than I can put into words. Much thanks also for the encouragement and for supporting my goals!

My thanks to David Hoof for feedback on individual stories and providing me much to consider as I edited the stories for publication.

I'm also appreciative to Mariana Amorim and Nicholas Raymond for making their photography available via Creative Commons licenses.

My thanks to Lori Felmey and Cynthia Ariel Evans for feedback on the cover as well as for their continued support of my efforts.

I offer my gratitude to all those who inspire me and encourage me to keep writing!

Betrayal

Meredith opened her brown eyes and looked around the unfamiliar room. She shifted in the dark brown micro-suede armchair. She had no business being there. She only agreed to come because Jonna asked, because Jonna needed her, because she didn't know how to say no, because she had no life. For all those reasons and none of them.

Silence permeated the space. She didn't see Jonna or Erik. She looked for a clock but found none. She glanced at her wrist. Empty. She left her watch at home.

Jonna had asked her to come along to keep her from making the same mistake as last time – the same mistake she always made when she tried to talk to Erik. Apparently, she failed.

"Jonna, where are you?" Meredith pushed her tall, lanky body from the armchair, shook her tingling arm, stretched her stiff neck, and rubbed her hair over her short, spiky dark hair. She stepped around a stack of folders. She glanced down. They looked like files from the store.

She looked into the kitchen. No one. She passed the open bathroom door. No one. *Why bother?* She knew where they were even, but she avoided letting her mind entertain the thought. Still, she held out hope and looked in the guest room. No one. She sighed. Only one room left.

Meredith stopped outside Erik's door. She felt strange about knocking, but she wanted to go home. She refused to spend the night in Erik's house.

Every time Jonna came to talk to him about separating both personally and professionally, they ended up in bed. Well, maybe not exactly in bed, but in a naked embrace anyway. The breakup never happened.

Meredith came to help Jonna not fall for Erik's charm, but Erik talked so endlessly about nothing Meredith couldn't keep her eyes open. She fell asleep before Jonna got around to breaking up with him.

Meredith stood with fist poised to knock when Jonna quietly opened the door and slipped out. She averted her hazel eyes but not before Meredith saw a flash of defiance in them. "Let's go."

"Jonna."

"I don't want to talk about it." Jonna tugged her clothes over her well-proportioned curves and glanced up at Meredith's face.

"We have to. Jon, you've got to do this and soon. He's going to destroy everything you've worked so hard to achieve."

"I know, Mere, honestly I do." She shook her brown hair over her face, grabbed Meredith's arm, and pulled her toward the door. "I can't. Not now. Let's get out of here."

Jonna fumbled in her purse for her keys. Finding them, she pushed them into Meredith's hand. "You drive. We had a couple of drinks after you fell asleep."

"Sure. No problem."

As Meredith backed Jonna's midnight blue Toyota Camry

out of Erik's driveway, she asked. "Have you ever considered talking to him in a restaurant?"

"He hates restaurants."

"What?" Meredith glanced over at Jonna. "You can't be serious."

Jonna shrugged. "That's what he says. We've only gone to a restaurant once."

"In three years?"

Jonna nodded. "He felt so anxious, he became physically ill. We left before the entrée arrived. Took the food to go. And he still refused to eat it."

"That's just weird. You've got to find a public place to end this. It's not working and you know it. It's draining you in too many ways."

"Maybe there's another solution."

"Another solution? Get real, Jonna. He's going to destroy your store. He's useless as a boyfriend."

"Not useless." She smiled. "He's great in bed."

"Is good sex worth everything else in your life?"

"Of course not."

"Do you love him?"

Jonna looked out the window without speaking.

"Oh, damn. Do you?"

"I don't know. We've spent three years together. We've had some good moments. Things used to be good with us. We had plans."

"Jonna, you know he's been using your business to hide...."

"Don't say it. I don't know anything for sure. I suspect something. He's good to me. He's always supported my...."

"What more evidence do you need?"

"You don't understand. He doesn't mean any harm. He just gets... caught up in things."

3

Meredith didn't reply. She clenched her jaw and focused on driving. Jonna turned on the radio and switched through the stations.

***

The next morning Jonna stepped into her bookstore. She loved this place. Spending her days surrounded by books was her dream come true. She'd been an avid reader for as long as she could remember. The bookstore offered her a forum to get paid to encourage people to read. She took a deep breath. Something about the scent of a room filled with books comforted her. She pulled the drying fresh flowers from the vase beside cash register and replaced them with daisies she'd picked up from the florist a few doors down. He put a display of her books and her business cards by his cash register and provided her with fresh flowers every few days. She straightened his business cards and smiled. The subtle hint seemed to work. Customers often went from one store to the other buying both books and flowers.

A glance at her watch reminded her she had another hour before the store opened. She placed her book bag, purse, and coat in the office. For the next few minutes she walked around the store straightening displays and replacing books left on tables. Along the way she made mental notes about displays that needed changed or updated. She refilled the newsletter bin and the stack of bookmarks with the store logo and website on the table by the door.

The busy work allowed Jonna to avoid what she didn't feel quite ready to face. She looked around. She sighed, squared her shoulders, and headed to her office. She had to figure out why the books refused to balance. She wanted it to be a mistake. She wanted it to stop pointing at Erik. She needed to find an explanation.

Erik had handled the bookkeeping when she went to North Carolina to handle her mother's estate a few months earlier. Jonna hadn't seen her mother since she three days after her fifth birthday. Her mother had dropped her at her grandma's house when she left with her new husband – a man who had no interest in raising another man's child. Her father had died in a car accident nine months earlier.

She loved living with her grandma – one of the most wonderful women she'd ever known, but that did little to erase the sting of being abandoned by her mother. She'd been surprised when the lawyer called to say her mother left her everything she owned. The lawyer also informed her that her mother's husband died a little over a year earlier.

When she arrived at the lawyer's office, he looked at her with compassion in his blue eyes and handed her a letter as soon as she sat down. "She asked that you read this before we talk about the will." She stared him. His dark hair was just beginning to gray around the edges, and he looked like he'd once played sports, football probably, but no longer kept up the workouts necessary to maintain that kind of physique. He stood and left the room.

> Dear Jonna,
> I came by your store the other day. I don't think
> you recognized me. I bought a copy of *The Little*
> *House* because I remember it was your favorite
> when you were little.

Jonna remembered the lady. Her voice sounded sad when she said. "This was my daughter's favorite."

Jonna replied. "Mine, too. Your daughter has good taste."

"Yes, she does." A tear threatened the older lady's eyes as she turned to leave.

Jonna turned back to the letter.

> I wanted so much to tell you it was me, but I felt I
> didn't have the right. You seemed so happy, and I
> didn't want to upset you. Your pained expression
> when I mentioned the book made me feel so bad.
> I'm sorry, honey. I messed up, and I never knew
> how to set it right.
> Please follow your dreams.
> Above all, be happy.
> I always loved you. I know that's probably hard
> for you to believe.
> Love,
> Mom

Jonna walked over and opened the lawyer's door. She smiled at him and nodded. He walked back in the room. Once he settled behind his desk, she looked down at the letter again and then at him. "I don't know what to say."

"There's no need to say anything. Your Mom was comfortable but not rich. When she knew it was close to time, she sold her house and car, moved into an assisted living facility, and put everything she owned in a trust. She made you the only beneficiary. As soon as the paperwork clears, it will be yours."

"You said she knew."

"Yes, she had pancreatic cancer. They caught it too late for treatment to do any good."

"Oh." She averted her eyes. "I hadn't talked to her since I was a child."

"I know. Leaving you was her only regret."

The bell above the door jingled as Meredith entered the store. Jonna snapped back to the present. The Quickbooks report in front of her made no sense. Maybe if she could manage to concentrate on it for more than five minutes, she'd figure it out.

Meredith stuck her head in the door. "Hey, Jonna, I'm here." She glanced at the desk. "Going over those reports again?"

"I have to figure this out. I have to find the actual problem or come tax time I'll be screwed."

"I see. So you've quit trying to clear Erik?"

Jonna looked at her. She sounded like she wanted Erik to be guilty. "If I clear him in the process, so much the better."

Meredith shook her head and left. Jonna stared after her. *Why did Meredith want Erik to be guilty? Did she hate him that much?*

***

Meredith stood behind the cash register in the front of the store. Her hands shook. Jonna should just leave well enough alone. If she had just let Meredith do her job, none of this would be happening. Jonna was usually too busy to read the reports so closely. Last month though, she and Erik had a huge fight, the kind of fight that involved shouted, embarrassing words that could never be retracted and slamming doors. Jonna worked late into the night several nights to avoid him. She excused her new attentiveness to the finances by saying she wanted tax time to be less stressful. If Jonna had stuck to her habits, the problem would've been resolved well before she noticed.

Erik sauntered into the store. "Hey, Mere, what's up?"

"Jonna's reviewing the books again." She glanced up. She couldn't deny he was handsome with his svelte body, spiky blonde hair, mischievous green eyes, and inviting smile. If only he didn't strike her as so wrong for Jonna. She didn't even know why. She just knew he would only bring trouble to Jonna's life.

"Oh." He stopped halfway across the store and turned back. "She's in a terrible mood then."

"Well, not a good one for sure."

"Maybe I should come back later."

A voice cut through the store. "Erik, come back here."

He jumped and turned to look at Jonna's face. Jonna smiled but her eyes remained hard. "Please."

***

Jonna watched Erik walk toward her. He smiled. She wanted to smack him. "Hey Jonna. How's life?"

"It's been better." She sat down and pointed to an old pine kitchen chair with a brown leather padded seat. "Have a seat."

He sat on the edge of the chair jiggling his right leg and looking past Jonna to the computer screen. "So what's going on with the numbers, Jon?"

"I wish I knew, Erik." She sighed. "I keep reviewing the books. There's a large amount of money missing. I'm trying to discover where it went and how."

He stood and leaned toward the computer screen. "Can I help? Maybe if we start with how you noticed the missing money."

"Erik, you misunderstand. I'm not asking for your help."

"Then what..." His voice trailed off. "Wait a minute. Are you saying... Do you think..."

Jonna sighed. "I don't know. You have access to the accounts and the inventory."

"What? I don't know what you're talking about."

"Erik, you place orders, pay bills, and return merchandise. That gives you access to both income and expenses."

"Not really." He leaned forward. "You have to sign off on everything I do."

Jonna sat back. "That's just it. The numbers of what I've approved don't match the number in the accounts even when I account for unresolved items."

"So someone is getting to money and inventory before it gets to the accounts."

"That's how it looks."

"Have you talked to Meredith?" Erik asked. "Maybe she can point you in the right direction. She knows about this kind of stuff, doesn't she?"

"Yeah. She studied accounting. I asked her. She couldn't figure it out either." Jonna closed her eyes and sat back in her chair. "Erik, I run a small bookstore. I have two employees, Meredith and Jason. The only other people who ever work here are you and me. Jason's barely able to work the register. I highly doubt he could steal in such a concealed way."

"No kidding. Jason's only here three afternoons a week. He never takes money to the bank and his only access to inventory is what's already been entered in the computer." He paused. "That leaves Meredith and me unless you have another personality you've neglected to introduce to me." Erik nudged her elbow.

She gave a half smile. "Funny, but not now."

"Jon..."

"Don't. I need to focus. I have to figure this out."

"Let me take a look."

"I can't do that."

"Sometimes a fresh pair of eyes..."

"Exactly." She reached for the phone. "Thanks. But it can't be yours or Meredith's. Could you go now, please?"

She waited until he left the room and dialed. Meredith appeared in the door while she listened to ringing on the other end. Erik looked mad. "Did you break…"

Joanna waved her away. "Not now, Meredith." She turned her back to the door and left a message. "Tom, it's Jonna. I know it's been a while since we talked. I need to talk to you about a business issue. Please call me at the store. Thanks."

***

Meredith wandered around the store straightening books that didn't need straightened. She glanced toward the two customers in the store occasionally but didn't offer either help.

Jonna wasn't crying on her shoulder. She wasn't looking for reassurance. She refused to her offer to talk – dismissed her, actually.

Erik had definitely left unhappy – not angry or dejected but unhappy. There hadn't been any shouting or crying. He hadn't looked like someone who'd just been dumped. Jonna looked more determined than upset. *What was it going to take to break them up? He was so bad for Jonna. When was she going to see that?*

She looked at the closed office door. *What was Jonna doing now? Who did she call?*

"Ma'am." A voice pulled Meredith out of her thoughts. Meredith looked at a slightly overweight middle aged woman who wouldn't stand out in a crowd even if she chose to wear something more interesting than the navy jogging suit she currently wore.

"Yes, how can I help you?"

"Do you have any books on yoga?"

"Of course." She turned toward the back of the store.

"This way, ma'am."

The woman found two books and made her way to the cash register as Meredith was ringing up the other customer's order.

Meredith looked around the empty store, picked up a book of poetry, and settled on the barstool behind the cash register. She looked up from the book when Jonna came out of her office carrying her briefcase. "Meredith, I'll be back in a couple of hours. I've got an appointment. Call my cell if you need me."

"Okay."

***

Twenty minutes after Jonna left the bookstore, she knocked on Tom's office door before she opened it. He looked up. "Come on in, Jonna. My receptionist had an appointment this morning, so no one is manning the front desk." He leaned back in his chair. "It's been a long time. How are you?"

She stretched her hand toward him. He rose to shake it. Then he stepped around the desk instead. "That's no way to greet an old friend." He hugged her tightly.

She hugged him back for a moment, then stepped out of his embrace. "I'm okay. How's Shayla?"

He cleared his throat. "Fine. We just spent a week in France. Life's been pretty good."

"Glad to hear it."

"Look, about what happened…"

"Tom, let's not go there. Shayla didn't understand our friendship. Not many women would've. Hell, I'm not sure I would've if I'd been in her place." She looked into his deep brown eyes. They hadn't changed. They still expressed every emotion that crossed his mind and never lost their warmth.

He smiled, his white teeth glowing against his olive skin. "That's very understanding of you."

She looked down at his name plate – marble and brass – Thomas Martinez, CPA. "Tom, I appreciate you wanting to make me feel better, but I'm fine. I called you because I need to hire you to look over my finances. I need someone I can trust."

"What's going on?"

She pulled out a stack of files and a thumb drive. "Something is off in my accounts. The money and inventory…"

He put up a hand. "Jonna, let me take a look without knowing more. If I have preconceived notions about what you've discovered, I may miss something important." He reached over to take the files from her. She hesitated. "J, I'm good at what I do."

"It's not that. I know you are. You're the best CPA I know. That's why I called you." She shifted. "I'm a little concerned about what you'll find. It could change my life."

He studied her face a moment. "These things generally do. But it's better to know."

She handed him the copies. "How does this work? Do we go over them together?"

"No. It's best if I go over everything without you present. If you brought everything I requested, I should have all I need to find out what's going on. I'll review everything, then we'll meet to go over my findings."

"Okay. Feel free to call me if I missed anything you asked for or you have questions."

"Of course. I know it's hard right now, but I need you to trust me. I do forensic audits quite frequently."

***

When Jonna arrived back at the store, she noticed tension emanating from Meredith. "Mere, I'm sorry. I know you like to take your lunch at eleven-thirty to avoid the rush. It couldn't be helped. Business appointment. Only time I could get in. Take an extra half hour. I've got the store."

"I can wait if you want to talk."

"Not now. I need to think. Go to lunch. You must be starved."

"What about yours?"

"Grabbed a sandwich on the way back." She held up her hand. "Skip the lecture. I know fast food is bad for me."

***

Meredith left. The knot in her throat stopped the question she didn't want to ask. She swallowed hard. Jonna had been her best friend since high school. *How could she suspect... But then, why wouldn't she?* It wouldn't be the first time Meredith proved deceptive.

***

Jonna watched Meredith leave unaware her thoughts mirrored Meredith's. She didn't want to suspect Meredith, but Erik seemed genuinely surprised when she talked to him earlier. Meredith repeatedly pushed her to suspect on Erik from day one. On the other hand, Erik had pointed at Meredith.

Four customers roamed around the store. Jonna settled her things behind the counter and offered her help. A mom bought books for her four children – two books per child. Another lady bought two books on day trading. The third, a man, bought a stack of mysteries. The last customer, a woman who asked a bunch of questions, took two stacks of books to one of the easy chairs and spent forty-five minutes looking through them left without buying anything or returning the books to the shelves.

Alone in the store, Jonna returned the books to their various shelves around the store. The woman certainly had myriad interests. Then she turned her attention to the day's sales, counted the money in the cash register, and checked the computer for the day's inventory levels. Other than a penny or two, she didn't notice any discrepancies. She stared out the window and started to sketch out a design for a new window display, but her thoughts drifted.

Meredith made a huge mistake years earlier. It seemed silly to even consider it as a possible problem. Meredith was a different person now than the teenager she'd been when arrested for stealing. Even then, it had only been to get money to feed her brothers and sisters when their Dad died and their Mom lost herself in an alcoholic stupor. She'd taken a couple hundred dollars and a few meals over a month from the restaurant where she worked. When the owner found out why, he'd dropped the charges and made her work off the debt. He'd also taken her mother to Alcoholics Anonymous and helped her get sober. Desperation had driven her to it before. Meredith hadn't mentioned any problems, but then again she didn't the other time either - until she got caught.

The bell above the door chimed as a customer entered. Jonna smiled, "May I help you?"

"No thanks. Just looking around."

Joanna retrieved a sketch from her book bag and studied it. She still wasn't happy with it. The store planned to host a group book signing in a month, so she needed to figure out the best way to do a display for twenty authors. She moved to the front of the store and jotted down some notes as she stood in front of the table facing the entrance. She closed her eyes to envision the books on the table. She also needed to add a poster and information about the event as well as the individual authors.

"Jonna?" Erik's voice broke her thought.

"Hi, Erik." She glanced at her watch. "Are you working this afternoon? I didn't see your name on the schedule."

"Jason and I are unpacking some books that arrived yesterday. I think they're for that big book signing next month."

"Oh, yeah. Of course. I knew they arrived"

"You seemed a little distracted there."

"Displaying books for twenty authors that provides equal publicity but creates interest for the public is a bigger challenge than I anticipated."

"Equality isn't the key. Attracting customers to the event is. All the authors should understand that."

Her eyes lit up. "It sounds so simple when you put it that way."

"But you have a need to always be fair." He kissed her cheek. "I think your customer is ready to check out."

She watched him walk to the inventory room across from her office as she returned to the cash register. She loved his saunter. She turned to her customer and smiled. "Sorry about the wait. How can I help you?"

*** *** ***

Over the next several days, Jonna tried to avoid thinking about what Tom might discover. She focused on preparing for store events and ways to garner more publicity for the store. She read books by local authors and reviews of books with upcoming release dates.

She avoided discussing the store's finances with both Erik and Meredith. She insisted on closing out the cash register at the end of each day and depositing the money herself. Her relationship with both her boyfriend and her best friend grew increasingly strained, but at least neither pointed a finger at the other one anymore.

***

Meredith needed to find a way out of the situation she'd created for herself. There was no way to fix her mistake. When Jonna found out, she would never trust her again. It wasn't like her actions hurt anyone. It was a temporary thing. She'd really been looking out for Jonna's best interests, but she wasn't so sure Jonna would see it that way. What she'd done wasn't really that bad.

Meredith's thoughts tumbled in her head as she returned books to their proper shelves. Really, she'd just wanted Jonna to see how wrong Erik was for her. Jonna had been her best friend forever. She knew her better than anyone, and she just wanted Jonna to be happy. *Would Jonna see it that way when the truth – the full truth – came out?* Maybe she would be better off to just tell Jonna the truth herself and take the consequences.

***

Jonna sat in her office typing an order for a small press. She'd read four books published by the press that she liked, so she decided to make an exception and order directly from the publisher since the press used a distributor with whom she was unfamiliar. She liked the part of her job that allowed her to give new authors and new presses a chance to succeed. She had scheduled a reading for one of the authors who would be passing through the area on his way to a larger city.

A knock on her office door drew her attention from the

order form. "Come in."

Meredith looked around the door. "Jonna, there's a local author here with her book."

Jonna glanced at her watch. "Damn! I'd forgotten. I need to finish this order. Tell her I'll be out in five minutes. Oh, and offer her a cup of tea or something."

***

While Jonna chatted with the local author, she saw Erik enter the store and head to her office. He didn't look around the store, and he stayed in the office. She agreed to take a few of the author's books on consignment and arranged a second meeting to discuss planning an in-store event with several local authors. She tried to discreetly watch her office for Erik's exit as the author described her series.

After she left the author to browse in the store, she marched over to her office and softly opened the door. She caught Erik looking through the filing cabinet. "Erik, is there something I can do for you?"

He kissed her quickly. "I was looking for the plans we drew up for expanding the shelf space in the store."

"Why?"

"I ran into a carpenter friend today who might be interested. I thought I'd show him what we discussed and get some feedback."

"That's my decision to make. Besides I'm not sure I'm ready to make that move."

He looked deflated. "I was only trying to help."

"I know. And I'd be happy to sit down and talk to your friend, but those plans are a goal to work toward."

"I thought things were going well."

"They are…" She let her voice trail off.

"Jonna, when are you going to trust me?"

"Don't ask questions you don't want the answers to?"

He sighed.

"Sorry, Erik. I'm not big on trust. If it helps, I trust you as much as I trust anyone."

"Nope, sorry, that doesn't really help. I thought I'd proven myself to you."

"It's not about that, and you know it."

"Do you still think I'm stealing from your store?" He paused until she looked at him. "I'm not."

Jonna's phone rang. She glanced down at the CallerID. It was Thomas. "Erik, this will have to wait. I need to take this call."

***

The next morning Jonna arrived at Thomas's office ten minutes before eight. The office didn't open until nine, but he'd asked her to come in at eight. She waited in the hall sipping a cup of coffee. She hadn't slept all night. All he'd told her was they needed to sit down and go over things but that he couldn't meet until the morning. Her cell phone rang. She sighed as she answered. "Hi, Meredith, didn't you get my message?"

"Yes, I did. You sounded funny. Is everything okay?"

"It's fine. I just have an appointment this morning. It's important."

"Is this about Erik taking that money?"

"Meredith, I don't want to discuss this other than to say I'm not so sure he did."

A long silence followed. "Jonna, I'm sorry. I know I shouldn't have accused him without evidence. It's just... Well, I've always thought you could do better."

"That's not your decision, Mere. It never was." She waved at Thomas as he walked down the hall. He carried a pale yellow box. "I've got to go. My appointment is ready for me."

"Okay. I think we need to talk when you get back to the store though."

"See you then." She hung up.

She felt like someone had punched her in the gut. Her instincts screamed she didn't want to hear what Meredith wanted to tell her.

She looked at Thomas. She saw sympathy, pain, and regret written across his face. No wonder he never won at poker. She closed her eyes and took a deep breath. "Hey Thomas."

He kissed her cheek. "Hello, Jonna. Let's get settled in my office. My secretary doesn't come in until nine. I wanted to discuss this with you in absolute private."

"I'm not going to like this, am I?"

"Probably not, Jonna. I've gone over the numbers a dozen times, and the results always came out the same."

"Honestly, Tom, I knew no matter what you found, I wasn't going to like it."

"It's never easy to be betrayed. And, I think you knew no matter what I found it was going to expose a betrayal of some kind. And, it would be by someone you care about a lot – possibly even love."

"Yes."

They sat at a table in the corner of his office. He opened the box. She saw her favorite pastries – chocolate croissants and cream horns from a local pastry shop. She smiled. "I thought I recognized that box."

"I thought a little treat might soften the blow."

"Just the fact that you remembered means a lot."

"Of course I remembered. We used to eat there every Sunday morning and talk about our Saturday night dates."

"Ah, yes. The good old days when our biggest worries were whether or not our dates went well enough to warrant a phone call."

"Well, that and our classes."

"Yes, but the dating continued after the classes ended."

"True enough."

He spread out some of the documents she had brought him. She noticed a number of sticky tabs in three colors: red, green, and blue. She picked up a croissant and bit into it. The dark chocolate filling was delicious against the buttery flakiness of the croissant. "Yum. Just what the doctor – oops, sorry, the accountant - ordered."

He laughed and picked up the second croissant in the box. "Okay, let's go over what I discovered. The person doing this was very clever. It was a frame job, which is probably why looking over the records confused you so much. I think someone wanted you to think someone else was stealing from you."

She closed her eyes. "What do you mean think?"

"We'll get there in a minute." He sipped his coffee. "Let me ask you, has anyone pointed the finger at anyone else?"

"Both the people I suspect pointed the finger at the other."

"I'm not surprised." He squeezed her hand. "Your relationship with both goes beyond professional."

"Well, yes, Meredith has been a friend forever. She's like family."

"Damn. I was hoping Meredith wasn't one of them. The other?"

"Erik. My current boyfriend."

"Current?"

"Long story. There have been problems for a while, but I've been determined to work them out. Then this happened, and I didn't want to antagonize him if he was behind this. I was afraid he might do something the store couldn't recover from."

"I see. Kind of a keep your enemies closer thing."

"No, not really. More of a 'I didn't want it to be him thing, and I didn't want another failed relationship', you know."

"Oh, Jonna, you've got to stop looking at life like that."

"Yeah. Yeah. Yeah. I know. But that's not the issue at hand."

"In a way it is. You see things through this filter that allows situations like this to happen."

"Thomas, it's not your job to fix me anymore."

"It never was, but that's not what I'm getting at. No matter what happened between us, I still care about you. That never changed."

"I know, and I understood. You loved – love – her. And, my mere presence created a problem in your relationship. I understand. Really I do. I'd been there. I just never cared about anyone enough to put their problem with our friendship first. You did. I've never blamed you for that."

"Never?"

"Okay. Maybe for a minute. It hurt. I'm human. You were my best friend." She looked away and blinked back a tear. "Come on, Thomas, that's not why I'm here. I need to protect my business, and you're the best at what you do. I hired you because I trust your accounting skills."

"And you trust me to have your best interests at heart."

"You always did."

"Thank you for recognizing that."

She waved away his gratitude. "The numbers."

"Okay, okay. You're right. We should resolve this, but I would like to have lunch soon and talk about being friends again."

"Thomas, I don't know if that's a good idea. Your wife..."

"knows I'm asking you. She's okay with it."

"Really?"

"Yes. She would actually like to sit down with you and see if you can forgive her for being so insecure."

"One thing at a time, please." She tapped the papers in front of him. "My store. I need to save it."

"Your book store is safe. The money isn't actually missing per se. Well, there is some missing, but not enough to force your business to close. Most of the money was moved around and most of the inventory that appeared to be missing was categorized incorrectly so it wouldn't show up on your reports. Someone did take some money from the accounts and put most of it back at some point. The majority of the money that appears to be missing though was just hidden again so it wouldn't show up on your reports. If I had to venture a guess, someone 'borrowed' some money and wanted to buy some time to put it back so they created this shell moving the money around and making it look like more was missing than they took."

"But that's stupid. More money missing would be more noticeable."

"Yes, but it would send you in the wrong direction looking for someone either trying to sabotage your business or embezzle from you giving the person time to put back the 'borrowed' money. My guess is they hoped they'd return the money, fix the accounts so it would look like there was either a glitch in the software or a mistake made in data entry that would make it all seem innocent. Or the other alternative is the person was actually setting someone else up to take the fall getting that person out of your life or at least out of the business. Once the damage was done, the missing money could be recovered from the accounts. It would then be too late to fix the relationship targeted." Thomas ran his hand through his hair, a nervous gesture she'd always found endearing.

"That's sure elaborate just to sabotage a relationship."

"Well, it's likely that the person responsible for taking the money stumbled onto the idea of framing someone else to sabotage the relationship after the whole scheme started."

"But Meredith and Erik both know if they were in trouble, I'd do anything I could to help them." Jonna blinked back a tear.

"Are you sure?"

"What?"

"Well, given Meredith's history, she does have major trust issues." Thomas's kept his voice soft. "And, you just told me things have been tense with Erik for a while."

"Okay, you have a valid point on both counts." She tapped the papers. "Were you able to determine who was behind this?"

"Well, since your identifiers didn't include names, you would have to make that final match, but, yes, I did figure out which login was creating the misdirection." He pulled out a stack of papers and showed her documentation of the actual missing money and the hidden money. She traced the identifiers he had given her. She sighed not wanting to believe what she saw. She would've felt the same way regardless of who betrayed her. "Damn, it was Meredith."

Tom leaned back. "I had a feeling."

"Really?"

"Yes." He studied her face. "Do you wish it had been Erik?"

"No. I wish it had all been a mistake, and that no one did anything intentional to hurt me." She continued scanning down the page. "Wait. What's this?"

He looked over. "That was the one anomaly I couldn't explain. This strange identifier that indicated someone not on your list did something."

"I never created this account."

"I don't think it matters. I couldn't find where any actual money was moved, hidden, or stolen with that identifier. It appeared here, shows two days worth of deposits, enters some items into inventory, and then disappears. I thought maybe you gave someone a temporary account in the system to help you get caught up during inventory or something."

"No, I've never hired a temp of any kind. It hasn't been necessary." She looked at it more closely for a minute before she pulled out her smart phone. She opened her calendar and pulled up the dates in question. She sat back and stared for a minute before closing her eyes.

"What is it?"

"I was out of town on the dates this occurred. I was dealing with my mother's estate. I have absolutely no idea what this is. I didn't think either Erik or Meredith had access to set up accounts on the system. I thought only I could do that. I don't know what this is."

"It may not matter. There doesn't seem to be anything beyond regular business going on with this account. You may want to take a look at your system though."

"Yes. I've also got to figure out what to do about Meredith. She's been my best friend forever. I can't bear to lose her yet I can't believe she would do this to me."

***

Meredith paced around the book store picking up stray books laying on tables, pulling wrongly shelved books from the shelves, returning books to the shelves, and straightening the books on the shelves as she went.

Anything to keep her mind occupied. She considered leaving - just getting in her car and driving away, far away.

She stayed though. She would face Jonna and explain her side of it. Even if Jonna didn't understand, she would do the right thing this time. Self-preservation had often driven her to do the wrong thing, but she refused to take the easy way out this time. She looked toward the door imagining that walking through it would cast her back in time allowing her to reverse her betrayal of Jonna, allowing her to make the right choice, allowing her to change everything.

Meredith sighed deeply as she returned to the cash register and started straightening the items on the shelves under the register. She sorted through a box of flyers, postcards and bookmarks tossing stacks of outdated material in the recycle bin. Authors were always sending materials to the store or dropping them off in person. She hated throwing promotional material away, but sometimes it was necessary, especially when the materials were for events like signings, readings or conferences. Sometimes though they found it necessary to toss material for books they'd quit stocking or had never stocked, especially if the book couldn't be special ordered. After all, the store needed to earn money and promoting work they didn't carry didn't earn money.

She pulled out another bin from under the front desk. Inside she found a stack of books authors had left for someone, preferably Jonna, to read to decide whether or not to stock the book. Jonna rarely made her decision based on actually reading the numerous books. She, Erik, or Jason spot read the books and made a recommendation to Jonna, who would then sometimes decide to give a book more attention before deciding whether or not to stock it.

Meredith sorted through the stack and found a few short

books. She settled down to skim a few pages from each one and write up short document with her thoughts for Jonna. She longed for a store full of customers to distract her from her thoughts, but the books would have to do.

Meredith finished making notes on the third book in her stack as the bell above the door chimed. She looked up. Erik walked in and waved at her. "Is Jonna here yet?"

"No."

"Do you know where she is?"

"I'm fairly certain she's meeting with Thomas this morning."

"Thomas?"

"Yes."

"*The* Thomas?"

"Yes, him."

"I thought she and he had a falling out."

"Not a falling out really. Thomas's wife didn't like them hanging out so much, well she was his girlfriend at the time. In the end, after several fights, Jonna ended the friendship. I don't know the details. I just know she said she had to walk away because his happiness was more important than keeping him in her life. I always thought there was more to it than that, but that was what she said. Then she refused to discuss it ever again."

"They never dated?"

"No, not as far as I know, and I would know if anyone would."

"Unless she opted to keep it a secret."

"True enough..." She looked toward the door. "What makes you think there was more?"

"Just the way she reacts on the rare occasion she mentions him or alludes to him. Her face kind of lights up but is filled with a mixture of happiness and sadness, kind of a longing."

Erik glanced toward the floor. "You know sometimes I wish she looked at me the way she looks when she mentions him."

Meredith looked at Erik and felt a little tug. Maybe she'd been wrong about him. Maybe he felt more than he let on. Maybe he just hid his feelings. He always appeared so aloof. Jonna needed someone who enveloped her love. She stifled a sigh and watched him for a minute. "I don't know what to tell you, Erik. He's married now. She's with you. That has to mean something."

"I suppose." He tilted his head toward the door. "I need to talk to her. I guess I can inventory some books while I wait."

Meredith nodded to the customers, a mother and young son from the look of it, as she returned to the register. A few more customers wandered in. She glanced up every few minutes as she sorted through the stacks books organizing them by topic and level of projected interest. She didn't want the customers to feel watched but wanted them to see her availability if they had questions. Sometimes there was a fine balance between appearing alert and appearing suspicious.

* * *

Jonna sat in her car and watched the store. She hated what she had to do. She hated being put in this position. She wanted to pretend all was well. She wanted to walk through those doors as if she didn't know what she knew. She wanted to be transported back in time before all this happened. She wanted her trust in Meredith and Erik restored.

But it didn't really matter what she wanted. Reality forced her to take notice. These accounting problems could have cost her her store had she not discovered them, and her store meant too much to her to allow that to happen. Yet, Meredith and Erik had been her strongest supporters personally and professionally for as long as she could remember. She reminded herself that Erik hadn't done anything wrong. He'd been framed. Yet, she quickly added him to the suspect list when the occasion arose, and she didn't like what that said about her feelings for him. She sighed.

She prepared herself to face both Meredith and Erik. The next few hours would change everything – her business, her responsibility, her life. She watched Erik enter the store and come back out. He went next door and came out carrying two boxes and looking triumphant. He entered the book store again. She watched Meredith meet him at door and rescue a tipping box. Then she watched a series of customers enter the store. She used their entry as an excuse to procrastinate going into the store and dealing with the situation at hand.

Finally, she took a deep breath. Maybe she should wait until closing to deal with it anyway. Dealing with it between customers or with customers in the store wouldn't be good for the book store. Customers didn't want or need to know about the store's problems.

Jonna stepped through the doors. Meredith looked up with a smile, but her face quickly shadowed. Jonna nodded at Meredith and headed to her office.

Erik sat in her office, humming along to the radio as he entered books into inventory. He looked up and smiled as she entered. "Hey, Jonna, how's your day going?"

She smiled but fought back sobs. She blinked hard to keep from crying. "To be perfectly honest, Erik, not so good."

He stopped and turned to look at her. "Want to talk about it?"

"Maybe in a minute. Right now I'm still trying to assimilate it."

"Okay." He paused, picked up the next book and started processing it. "Meredith said you've been talking to Thomas."

She stared at him. After a moment's silence, she sighed. "That's true. How did she know?"

"I don't know. She didn't say." He looked at her. "Are you... Is he... Are the two of you... Do I need to be worried?"

"What do you mean? Worried about what?"

"Us."

"Huh? Are you nuts? Thomas and I never... I'm not discussing my relationship with Thomas with you. He's a forensic accountant. He's been going over the store's books to see if he can find the problem I couldn't figure out."

"Oh." Erik stayed quiet for a long minute. "You went to him for help." His tone contained a combination of question and accusation that Jonna didn't appreciate.

"Yes, I did. He's the best forensic accountant in town, and he's a friend. I knew I could trust him."

"But you didn't trust me." Again that combination of question and accusation.

"No, I guess I didn't. I told you before. The evidence pointed toward you."

"You should've trusted me."

"Maybe."

"Maybe?" He slammed the book down on the desk. "Maybe? Are you kidding me? We're dating. If you can't trust me, why are you still with me?"

She paused for too long, but the words refused to be said. In that pause she realized what she'd known for quite a while. Their relationship was over. Instead of answering his question, she changed the subject. "Did you create a temporary account while I was dealing with my mother's estate?"

He looked confused. After a minute, he let out a slow deliberate breath. "Yes, we got in a large shipment you'd ordered before you left. I needed help with the data entry, so I created an account for Jason. It was temporary, and I removed his privileges immediately after the project was complete. Did that somehow create the accounting problems?"

"No, but it added to the confusion. You should've told me."

"I didn't even think about it." He paused. "I actually forgot all about it. Sorry. I didn't realize it even mattered."

She nodded. She had no words. She really didn't want a scene while customers shopped in the store, so she stared at her fingernails.

A heavy silence layered between them. She listened to the clacking noise of his fingers on the keyboard and closed her eyes while she reminded herself to inhale, exhale, inhale, exhale until the words blurred together in her thoughts.

After he finished entering the stack of books next to him, he turned to her. "You never answered my question."

"I know."

"Well?"

She sighed and looked at the wall. She really needed to paint her office. Maybe she should go with something vibrant and energetic. She shook her head. "I want to say because I love you."

"You want to say it, but you can't."

She shook her head and fought back tears.

"Then, I'll make this simple. I'm done. I can't do this anymore. You'll never be able to love someone until you admit to yourself how you really feel. Until you deal with all those closed places in your heart and your fear of abandonment. Until you admit that the person you really love is…"

She put up her left hand. "Stop right there. Love? Are you serious? We've never discussed love. You've never said you love me. I've never said I love you."

"What? Of course we have."

"No, we haven't. It's not worth arguing about."

"You're right. It's not. The reality is you don't trust me. We're over."

"Okay. So we're over."

He stared at her. "That's all you have to say?"

She let out a slow breath. "Yeah, I think it is."

Erik stood. He walked to the door. He stopped with his hand on the knob. "You know I spent our entire relationship trying to prove something to you but I never really knew what I was trying to prove. It seemed like the rules changed every time we got close to being truly intimate on anything more than a sexual level."

"I don't know what to say, Erik. I really don't. I wish I did."

Jonna watched him walked out the door. She searched in her heart to feel something, but she didn't unless emptiness counted. The conversation hadn't gone as she'd hoped, but it had gone the way it needed to go. She ran her hand through her hair and looked at the stacks of books Erik had entered into inventory. He wasn't a bad guy. He just wasn't the right guy for her. Better to learn that now than later.

She picked up the next book on the stack and picked up the inventory entry right where Erik left off. Life went on. Nothing had really changed except Erik would no longer be part of her life. Not that he'd been that much a part of her life since her suspicions of him began. She wondered if maybe she'd used this as an excuse to push Erik away. She could've trusted him. She could've talked to him. She could've given him the benefit of the doubt. She chose not to, and that choice dictated everything that lead to this moment.

She listened to the noise of customers entering the store, browsing, shopping, making small talk with Meredith, and making purchases. She inventoried the new arrivals, updated the financials from the previous few days, and placed a new order. She glanced at her watch. It was still too early to talk to Meredith and risk a scene in the store. She started cleaning off her desk processing the five minute tasks that she tended to procrastinate, throwing away outdated action items, and organizing larger tasks for a time when she could give them more attention. Then she turned her attention to the shelves in her office. By closing time, her office looked like a professional organizer had tackled it. Not only did the office look better but Jonna felt more focused.

She left the door open all day, so she could hear the activity in the store. She hadn't stepped out of her office though. She hadn't wanted to see Meredith. She barely managed to control her anger. She felt too betrayed. But she also didn't want to create a scene while customers were in the store. That would be bad for business.

Meredith hadn't come near her office all day either. Meredith must have realized what she'd discovered. She sat back in her chair and took a deep breath. Jonna listened as Meredith locked the front door, closed out the cash register, and straightened up the store. Finally, Meredith knocked on her door. "Hey, Jonna, you okay?"

"Yes, Meredith, please come in and sit down."

Meredith stepped inside and handed Jonna a stack of

papers. "Here are my comments on the books from the bin. I recommended quite a few from this bunch."

"Okay." Jonna took the papers and placed them in her inbox. "I'll look them over in the next day or so."

"Haven't seen much of you today." Meredith sat down. "Hope everything is all right."

"It's not, Meredith." Jonna took a deep breath and looked at Meredith's face. "We need to talk."

"I know."

"I had Thomas Martinez take a look at the store's financial records."

"Why?"

"Because he's the best forensic accountant around."

"But given your history…"

"He's the best, and I trust him. That's not what we need to discuss though."

Meredith closed her eyes and turned her head to face the floor. "I saw Erik leave earlier. He didn't look happy."

"Stop deflecting, Meredith."

"I just wondered if you two…"

"It's not your business, Meredith."

"I'm your friend."

"Meredith, stop. I know the truth. Thomas found what you did. He showed me this morning. I just want to know two things. Why would you steal from me? Why frame Erik for it? Please help me understand, Meredith."

Meredith raised her head, faced Jonna, and started to speak.

"I recognize that look, Meredith. Please no lies and no excuses. Just tell me straight out."

"Fine. The truth. I needed the money. I made a few bad decisions and was in danger of losing my house and my car. I thought I could pay back the money before you discovered it was missing."

"Why frame Erik?"

"Because he was bad for you—and in case you noticed the money was missing. To buy myself some time. I didn't want to lose our friendship."

"Meredith, you should've talked to me about your money problems. We could've worked something out. We were friends. You stole from me. And framing Erik was low, really low. No matter what you thought of him."

"Are you going to call the police?"

"No, but I probably should. I know you returned all the money, so I won't call the police."

"But I'm fired."

"Yes, you're fired."

"What about our friendship?"

"Friends don't steal from friends. I can't forgive this, Meredith. I've thought about it all day, and I just can't. You need to leave now."

"Okay, I understand." Meredith swallowed hard as tears threatened the corners of her eyes. "Can I just say one thing first?"

"Sure, go ahead."

"I'm really, really sorry, Jonna. I wish I could go back and make a different decision. I wish I could make it up to you. I would like a chance to fix our friendship."

"I can't do that, Meredith. I can't trust you again. It's not like this is the first time."

"I know, but I had to say it. Maybe someday…"

Jonna looked at her former friend and all she felt was pity. Even the anger was gone. "No, Meredith, not someday. I don't want you to hold on to a hope that doesn't exist. Just go live your life and don't ever treat a friend like this again."

Meredith stood and walked out. Jonna dropped her head

on her desk as soon as she heard the front door close and let her tears fall.

The bell over the front door chimed alerting her when someone entered the store. Meredith must not have locked it when she exited. Jonna stood, wiped away her tears, squared her shoulder, and stepped out into the store. "I'm sorry, we're clo..." She began and stopped as she saw who stood inside the doorway.

"I thought you might need a friend tonight, JonJon."

"Thomas, what a surprise."

"How did it go?"

"Well, I lost my boyfriend and my best friend all in the same day, but I expected as much."

"Are you okay?"

"Not really, but I will be."

"Let me buy you a drink."

"Shouldn't you be getting home to your wife?"

"About that... I lied... Well, not so much lied as wasn't ready to face the truth myself.... We're separated. Have been for a while. I guess I kind of hoped we'd work things out. We tried to, but sometimes you just have to face the truth. And, the truth was she and I were never right for each other."

"I tried to tell you that a long time ago."

"I know, but I couldn't have the woman I wanted."

"Why not?"

"She didn't love me like that."

"What are you talking about?"

"She only wanted to be friends." He took a step closer to her. "She didn't believe in relationships."

"Who are you talking about, Thomas?" Jonna asked. Her heart pounded. She had dreamed about this exchange so many times. She needed him to say the right words, to actually say them out loud.

"Who do you think?"

"Thomas…"

"Jonna, I've been in love with you since forever. The moment you walked into my office, those feelings flooded back and I knew I had to tell you this time. I knew…"

She tiptoed and kissed his lips. "I love you, Thomas. I was just so afraid you didn't feel the same way about me that I couldn't risk our friendship by telling you. Having you be my friend was better than not having you in my life at all."

"But you let me just walk away."

"I thought you were happy. I thought she could give you everything I couldn't, and I didn't want to stand in the way of your happiness."

"And yet you did."

"What?"

"You are my happiness, Jonna."

"Oh, no, don't put that pressure on me. I can't be your happiness."

He laughed. "That's not what I meant, sweetheart. I simply meant that having you in my life makes me happy. And, I am willing to risk everything to pursue a relationship with you, to pursue a chance at real happiness with you."

He put his arms around her and pulled her close, hugging her and then kissing her slowly. She felt her body press toward him relaxing into his embrace. She gasped as his lips left hers. He looked into her eyes and smiled. "So what do you think?"

"I'm all in."

He smiled. "Good. How about that drink?"

"Why don't we make it dinner instead? I've not eaten since those pastries this morning, and I have a feeling I'm going to need all the energy I can get."

The Diamond

Justin looked out the small window of his grandfather's hunting cabin. The light filtered through the trees and shimmered on the leaves like diamonds. Actually, it was his cabin, but he would always think of it as his grandfather's. His grandfather surprised him a few years back when he willed the place to him, especially since Justin hadn't hunted since his thirteenth birthday. The cabin provided a wonderful refuge, nowhere near luxurious, but a refuge nonetheless.

The rustic one room cabin contained bunk beds against the far wall, a wood stove in the middle of the room, and the old oak table and matching four chairs his grandfather built before Justin's father's birth. Justin dropped the heavy piece of faded brown canvas back over the window. The only light in the room emanated from a kerosene lamp. He lifted a pan of water from the stove.

He poured the boiling water into a blue enamel washtub and washed his unshaven face. Water dripped from the short stubble already softening into a beard. He rubbed the dark stubble on his face. He sometimes wished the cabin had running water, but he would never add it. He liked the nostalgia of "roughing it" on occasion. Besides, running water might make the place more appealing to Mikki.

He groaned. The mere thought of her threatened to ruin a perfectly good morning. He came to the cabin to get away from her.

He pulled a pair of jeans and a flannel shirt over his long johns. His tall, lean frame didn't take the cold autumn air of the mountains well. Suddenly, for a quick moment, he wondered how thermal underwear came to be called long johns. He brushed his brown hair with an old, battered brush with half the bristles missing and studied the lines and dark circles forming around his deep blue eyes. Oh, well, no jury needed influenced, no girlfriend needed impressed, no one would see him here in the woods. Even the wildlife kept its distance. Animals sensed energy, and his certainly felt repellent, even to himself.

He slipped on a faded orange and brown plaid jacket probably left behind by his grandfather judging from its age and size. He wrapped it around his torso with room to spare and chuckled. His grandpa had always held a large presence in both size and energy. Justin felt a small pang of longing to hear his grandpa impart some wisdom on his current situation.

Outside, he grabbed the ax from a stump by the cabin and chopped up a stack of old logs piled to the right of the cabin. He needed firewood. Good thing the logs were already there when he arrived because he had no idea how to cut down a tree or even how to choose the right one to cut for firewood.

Perhaps he should have accepted at least one of his grandfather's or father's invitations to spend a weekend at the cabin. They both asked often enough, but he'd always been too busy. He always prioritized something else as more important; study to get a scholarship, homework to keep his grades up in college, then law school, and then proving himself as an associate in a law firm, and then he'd had partnership to earn.

He raised the ax above his head and brought it down with all his force splitting the next log in half. He felt the force of his strength, his regrets, his thoughts, his effort vibrate through his arms into his shoulders, up his neck, and finally come to rest in his head.

He couldn't stay at the cabin much longer. He had cases to get back to and a life to… to what? He didn't know. He stacked the last piece of wood on the pile beside the house and went inside to make coffee. He stoked the fire and sat down with his sketchpad. He hadn't even allowed himself to think about his love of sketching, painting, and drawing since… well, far too long. In the three days since he'd come to the cabin he had filled two sketchpads. He started his third. Most of the pictures needed a lot of work, but he enjoyed exploring his passion.

He buried his art years earlier when his Dad sat him down and explained that art would be a hard life and he probably wouldn't be successful until after he died. He pointed out that Justin liked fine things and needed a profession that would support the lifestyle he wanted. From that day, his fourteenth birthday, he had put his art in a box and poured all his attention and energy into his schoolwork.

He watched Mikki's face flow from his pencil onto the paper. He loved her, but he wasn't going back. He needed to purge her from his system. That's why he'd come up here. Forgiving her felt impossible. His pencil continued to move on the paper as his mind drifted back to that last day with Mikki.

They should be on vacation. They should be sleeping late,

spending the day lying on the beach sipping daiquiris and dancing the night away. Instead, the nonrefundable tickets to the Bahamas remained under the seat of his Explorer, wasted.

He had come home early so he could hide the engagement ring he planned to give her on the last night of their vacation. They started dating five years earlier and lived together for the past two. He planned to wait until the last night of their trip, but his excitement made him doubt he'd make it. He longed to see the surprise and delight on her face.

He saw her BMW as he pulled into the garage. She apparently decided to come home early, too. He removed the ring from his briefcase and slipped it into his jacket pocket. If he could figure out a way to distract her, he could slip it in with his shaving gear. She wouldn't look there.

He walked into the kitchen with a smile on his face. "Hi, Mikki, I'm home."

He heard no response.

He hung his jacket on the banister post before he bound up the stairs two at a time. He stopped outside the door to their bedroom. He heard her muffled voice. "I've got to go. He's home." Then a pause. "I'll call you when I get home." Another pause. "I'll tell him on our last night there. He deserves to enjoy this vacation." Yet another pause. "I really don't want to hurt him."

He opened the door. "Tell me now, Mikki."

"Oh, shit. I've gotta go. Justin just walked in." She hung up and turned to him. "Hi, Honey, you scared me. How was your day?"

"Tell me now, Mikki. What's going on?" He searched her hazel eyes as he braced himself to hear she loved someone else.

"It's nothing, really, Justin. It can wait until we get back. Trust me, it's better that way."

"No, Mikki, I want to know now. I don't like secrets. You know that. Out with it."

"Please, Justin, I just want us to enjoy our vacation."

"Tell me now." His voice so cold he saw her shiver.

"Come on, Justin" She pleaded. She fought back tears and played with the ends of her long blonde hair. "Let's just put it aside until we get back."

"Mikki, no, I can't, won't go on vacation with you just to wait for the ball to drop on my head, my heart." He shook his head.

She sank onto the bed. "Sit down then." Her voice echoed her defeat.

"No, I'll stand."

"Please don't hate me, Justin." When he only stared at her, she continued. "Remember last week when I was sick, when I had that bladder infection?"

He knit his brow in confusion. "Yeah."

"Well, I didn't really have an infection. I had an" She swallowed hard. "an abortion last Monday. I...."

"You what?" His brain refused to register her words. They were so far removed from anything he expected her to say.

"Justin, I'm sorry. I just don't know where our relationship is going. You work constantly. We've been together so long, and we never talk about the future...."

"I didn't think we needed to."

"I didn't want you to feel trapped, to grow to resent me or the baby. I just wanted to know you were with me because you loved me and you want to be, not because you felt obligated."

"Mikki, you should know me better than that. We've been

together long enough that I thought you knew how committed I am to this relationship."

"You never said."

"So you had an abortion without even talking to me about it?" He turned to look out the window and fought back tears. He'd always considered himself pro-choice, but that had been in the abstract. This was real. He had never even realized he wanted children. He hated being left out of the conversation.

"Justin, I...."

"We should have discussed it, Mikki. You should have given me a chance."

"I was afraid of what you'd say, of what you'd do."

"Of what? That I would leave? Well, if I had, you still could have had an abortion." He turned and looked her in the eye. "Or were you afraid that I'd want it? Damn, that's it, isn't it? I don't know you at all."

She stared at the floor. "Justin, I just didn't know what to do...."

"Mikki, I thought we had something real...." He stopped, turned away, turned back, opened his mouth as if to continue, turned away again and walked out of the room, out of the house, and got into his Explorer.

Justin drove while his thoughts churned and yet he couldn't put a coherent thought together. He didn't know where he wanted to go, but he had to get away from her before he did something regrettable.

He looked down at the drawing. Mikki's sad, devastated yes looked at him. He had drawn her just as she looked as he turned his back to her and walked out of the house, out of her life. He struggled with the idea of forgiving her. Her deception, her lack of trust in him, her lack of faith in their relationship created a fissure in his love for her that felt unfixable. He wondered if she had found the ring he'd left in the jacket he'd left hanging on the banister.

He needed to go back and face her soon. He wanted answers, but he felt unsure what questions to ask. She'd shut him out of one of the most crucial moments – decisions – of their relationship. He wanted to know why she told him absolutely nothing – not even a small hint, at least that he remembered. He searched his memories for something he missed but found nothing. Granted he'd been caught up in a couple of really big cases over the previous year at least, but still he'd always been there for her – at least he thought he had.

He lay the sketchpad down, stood and stretched. He could only stay at the cabin four more days. Even less if he decided not to return to the house he and Mikki shared.

The cabin represented a place to find the solitude he sought His thoughts refused to allow his solitude to find any peace.

His stomach growled. He needed to go into town for food. The trip took an hour to drive and then an hour back. Maybe he would just get a room for the night. He picked up his keys and turned to the door he'd left open when he came in earlier. A silent Miiki stood there. "Mikki." He stared at her in disbelief.

She held out her hand and opened it. She held the navy box with the diamond ring in it. He stared at the box as she opened it. The light glinted off the diamond just as the sun had off the trees earlier. "Justin, can we talk, please?"

"You found it."

"Justin, I…."

"Mikki, I can't do this now. There's…."

"Justin, you were going to surprise me."

"Yes, I was."

These words needed to remain unsaid. He wished they would stop. He wanted her to leave.

"I love you, Justin. Do you still love me?"

He paused. Well, he'd wanted the conversation to change. "I don't know, Mikki. I just don't know."

"I'm still the same person, Justin."

"But who is that person, Mikki?"

"Justin, I've always been strong and independent. You know that. You always loved that about me."

"Yes, but I never thought you could be so coldhearted, so selfish. You left me out of the whole thing."

"Justin, I'm sorry about that. I never meant to hurt you." She looked into his eyes. He felt her desire to find answers there. He possessed no answers for her to find. His own questions flitted through his mind as he searched her face for answers she appeared unable to provide.

"Why did you tell me at all?"

"You asked."

"You were going to tell me anyway."

"That's true."

"So why?"

"I don't know. It weighed on my mind. I felt the secret building a wall between us, and I couldn't live with that."

"And you didn't feel that wall before the abortion?"

"No, I didn't. Maybe I did, but I thought it would go away. I just couldn't live with it by myself. I needed you."

He laughed, the sound dry and humorless, almost harsh. "You needed me? Didn't you think about what this would do to me?"

"I thought you would understand."

He stared at her for a long moment. "Sorry to disappoint."

"Justin, I love you. Can't we work this out?" She stared

into his eyes with questions he couldn't answer.

"I don't know, Mikki. I can't look at you without thinking about what you did. I can't see you the way I used to. Right now all I feel is the pain and the disgust at your deception, your lack of faith in us, you lack of respect for me. Maybe that'll change with time, but right now all I know is I could be facing fatherhood, rejoicing in the possibilities, and celebrating our engagement. The engagement I've been planning for months. All that's shattered. Now I'm just left with this emptiness, this numbness, and the feeling I've lost all that matters."

"Justin, please, I love you."

"I'm not so sure you do, Mikki. If you loved me, truly loved me, you would've talked to me. We would've figured out what to do together."

"I made a mistake. I got scared and let my insecurities take over. I do love you. I promise." She choked back a sob. "I promise I will never shut you out again if you'll just give me another chance."

He shook his head. "I don't know if I can ever trust you again."

"Please, Justin, all I'm asking for is another chance."

"Then give me some time, Mikki. Let me come to terms with this." Then under his breath he added. "If I can."

She placed the diamond on the dining table and walked out the door. As he watched her leave, he wondered if he would ever be able to forgive her. Yes, he would eventually. If he didn't, he'd never be able to move forward with his life. After all, forgiveness offered him a way to find peace rather than inviting her behavior back into his life. Forgiveness didn't mean he ever had to love or trust her again.

He listened to her drive away and felt nothing. The diamond mocked him. Its sparkle reminded him he'd always associate it with deception revealed and possibility destroyed. He left the diamond on the table, locked the door, and left for town.

Fortress

Muriel stood in Ann Morrison Park in Boise, Idaho looking at the mountains. Her chest tightened as she wrapped her arms around her thin torso gripping her ribs on both sides. Those cold, dry, brown mountains trapped her here, trapped her inside herself. She wondered if she would ever feel free. Tears threatened to spill from the corners of her hazel eyes.

When she first saw those mountains, looking down from the plane window, they'd appeared to form a natural fortress to her. She'd found them comforting, beautiful even. A fortress appealed to her then. Those mountains protected her from the outside world, from her other life, from him.

But somehow, sometime they had turned on her. Left her feeling imprisoned. She struggled to take in a breath of clean, cool air as she used her index finger to secure a stray lock of brown hair that had escaped her ponytail holder.

She wanted, needed, to stop hiding, running, avoiding life, her past, her future, herself. She sighed as she glanced at her watch. Dale, the man who brought her to Boise, would be home from soon. She needed to go home. She didn't want him to worry. She smiled. The man she loved. He didn't trap her here. He never trapped her anywhere. Marrying him was the best decision she ever made.

Her gaze swept over the bare mountains again and up to the tree-covered mountains in the distance – the second, or outer fortress, she'd been convinced would keep her safe. Another fortress turned trap. She must break free from those traps. She needed to feel alive and safe again on the Boise side of those mountains or the other side.

She sacrificed far too much over the years in her need to protect herself. She needed to fight back, to fight for her life, to fight for herself.

Muriel folded the blanket she'd spent the last couple of hours sitting on while she read her journals from the past eleven years. Some had gaps of days, weeks, even months between entries, yet the journals documented her struggles with her demons.

She even found an entry complaining about her parents naming her after her paternal grandmother. Muriel sounded so old-fashioned. Growing up, the teasing had been relentless. She tried to forget the taunts used to manipulate her during the worst time in her life. "With a name like Muriel, no wonder you're such a prude. I'll break you of that prudishness, Muriel... Muriel, Muriel. You sure don't look like a Muriel."

Dale had played a supportive and instrumental role in the changes she'd sought. At the same time, she remembered every fight they fought as they faced the issues from her past. Most importantly, he never gave up on her.

She sighed. She needed to stop living in the past and embrace her future. Her dreams and goals rose to the surface as she experienced a new sense of confidence and hope. At times, embracing her confidence and strength still felt foreign, surreal even.

The weight of her past no longer crushed her. She finally felt ready to move past it, perhaps even to let it go. Still, she feared she suppressed and repressed what hurt too much to face. She'd done that before when her future brightened. Then her past crashed down on her when an unexpected reminder popped up in a magazine article written by the cause of her anxiety.

He possessed the gall to publish an article on building self-esteem for a women's magazine. If only people really knew him and the dark void his soul should inhabit. No one believed her when she tried to tell them all those years ago. She doubted anything had changed.

She loaded her things in the trunk of her silver Mazda 6.

A few drivers gave her strange looks as she drove home. She laughed and waved at them. Maybe they should turn up the volume, sing along, and car dance, too. Those simple pleasures felt liberating.

She arrived home to find Dale's Toyota Tundra parked in the driveway. So much for the two hours she planned to use to prepare for their celebration of the opening of her interior design firm. She planned to hold her formal grand opening after she returned from their trip where she planned to finally face her past and truly put it behind her.

Dale met her at the door with a worried expression on his clean-shaven face. "Honey, come and sit down."

His words jarred her. She searched his green eyes for answers. "What's wrong?"

"I got a call today from Aaron."

"So?" Aaron was Dale's brother and best friend. He'd also been the best man at their wedding. She sat down. "You talk to him every week."

Dale ran his fingers through his short dark brown hair.

"This was different. He called to warn us."

"Warn us?"

Dale fell to one knee, took her hands in his, and looked into her eyes. "Mark has been charged with harassing and raping a co-worker. He's planning to call you in as a character witness."

"What? Is he crazy?"

"I guess so." He shrugged.

"There's no way I can help his case. I'd rather rip my own tongue out than say anything to help that asshole."

"I know that, but remember he never believed he did anything wrong."

"Yeah, he probably thinks that this time, too."

"What are you going to do?"

"I don't know." She shrugged.

"There's more."

"What else could there be?"

"He published another article. This time he mentions you."

"You have to be kidding." She frowned and consciously slowed her breath by counting to eight. Eight always worked better for her than the cliché ten. "What could he possibly say about me? Anything from our therapy sessions falls under doctor-patient confidentiality. Surely, he wouldn't be stupid enough to talk about what he did to me."

"According to Aaron, it has something to do with the time when you worked for Mark before he convinced you that you needed therapy. He said he'd fax it over as soon as he gets home."

Muriel's shoulders slumped as she leaned forward, rubbing her hand over her brow. "Why can't I get past this? It all happened so long ago. Every time I think I'm moving on, it forces its way back into my life."

He gently caressed her arm. "It's a blimp, baby. It's not controlling you."

"Isn't it?"

"Our whole life revolves around this crap."

"No, it doesn't"

They sat in silence for a long moment. Finally, she quietly spoke. "Today I went to the park and went through the closure ritual we talked about."

"How did that go?"

"It went well. I thought I was ready for our trip. Now, I feel like my chest is about to explode."

"Panic attack?"

"I don't know." She thought a moment. "How did Aaron find out Mark wants to call me as a character witness?"

"He heard a rumor from a reliable friend at the court house. He wouldn't say who."

"So maybe it's not true."

"Maybe."

Muriel's entire body jerked as the fax machine kicked on. "That must be the article. Will you?" She tried to stop her hands from shaking.

"Sure."

Muriel dropped her head and covered her face with her hands. She heard rather than saw Dale come back into the dining room. The rustle of the paper indicated he held more than one sheet of paper. She kept her head down. She barely moved her hands away from her mouth. "What's it say?"

"Okay, it's not all that bad. He only uses your first name, and he talks about his theory that you were drawn to interview for the job in his office from an unconscious need for therapy to resolve issues you didn't consciously realize you had. The whole article revolves around how people are drawn to work in psychology, psychiatry, and social work due to unresolved, often repressed, trauma from their childhood."

"Actually, the theory itself holds some truth. I wonder what Mark's childhood trauma was."

"Do you really?" Dale sounded surprised.

"Not really, but a part of me would like to know why he does the things he does to women. I wonder if it might be easier to find closure if I could understand why."

***

Two mornings later she looked out the plane window at the brown mountains as the plane soared upward. Her heart pounded as she considered crossing that barrier. For years she'd feared crossing those mountains. Recent events proved those mountains only protected her in her mind. The mountains never created a real barrier that kept her past at bay, kept her pain away, kept her hidden.

Dale squeezed her hand. She squeezed his hoping to convey her gratitude to him.

***

Muriel met Dale about six months after her ordeal. She'd fought getting involved with him because she didn't trust anything good that came into her life. But he'd won her heart by being her friend no matter what she did to push him away. He never pushed her for anything more than a friendship. He offered her unconditional support; whether a shoulder for her to cry on, a meal to make sure she ate, a movie to make sure she laughed, or a caring ear to listen to her rant.

Gradually, almost without her notice, their friendship turned romantic. She loved Dale with all her heart and he loved her just as much. She never doubted his love even through her struggles to trust herself to trust.

***

As the plane descended toward Port Columbus International Airport, Muriel looked out at the city of Columbus, Ohio. It looked larger than she remembered. She closed her eyes and leaned her head against the headrest. Dale leaned over. "Are you sure you're ready for this?"

"It's time. Besides if that idiot is really planning to use me as a character witness, I need to do this while it's still on my own schedule, my own terms."

"Okay."

"Let's stick to the plan. We'll visit the places on our list, so I can face whatever emotions come up and move on."

"Right. We'll create a new association with each place once you've worked through the memories each place stimulates. I don't know if this is an approach the professionals recommend."

"Me either." She shrugged. "Counseling didn't help me though. I've come to this idea on my own because it's the only way I think I can get over my fears and live again."

After they checked in to the hotel in downtown Columbus, Muriel and Dale went for a walk in City Center Mall. Columbus housed no ghosts for her to face. Her demons lived a couple hours south in Portsmouth right where she'd left them all those years ago. She needed to relax before she started the hard work.

***

The next morning Muriel sat in front of the hotel window and stared out at the traffic below. She felt a hand on her shoulder. She jumped and turned. Dale stood beside her. "Good morning, hon! How long have you been awake?" He kissed her cheek.

"Since before sunrise. I couldn't sleep. I tossed and turned most of the night."

"I'm sorry, babe." He pulled her into his arms.

"Wasn't your fault. I just can't stop thinking about why we're here."

"We can go home if you don't want to go through with this."

"No, I need to do this. I'll just be glad when it's finally over."

"Breakfast first."

***

Three hours later they arrived in Portsmouth and parked downtown. Muriel wiped her sweaty hands on her pants and took a deep breath to calm her heartbeat. After several minutes that felt like forever, she calmed her anxiety enough to exit the car. The tension in her shoulders started to dissipate as they walked down a familiar but changed street. By the time they stopped for lunch at a small local restaurant that had been in business since well before she moved here right out of high school, she'd even managed to laugh a couple of times.

As they left the restaurant, Dale took her hand. "How are you doing? Are you ready for the next step?"

"I'm okay. I'm ready. So far it's been easier than I expected."

"That's because you're stronger than you think you are."

She smiled up at him. "Let's go to my old apartment building first."

His eyebrows lifted in surprise. "I thought you wanted to start with Shawnee State University."

"We can simply take a drive around campus. That should

suffice. Nothing happened on campus." She shrugged. "I just happened to be taking a couple of classes there when… Well, you know."

As Dale drove them around the campus, she smiled. "You know, I had some good times at this school. Not everything that happened in this town sucked."

Dale squeezed her hand. "It's good that you're remembering some happy things. Isn't that a step toward closure?"

"I think so. It's been so long since I've been able to remember anything good that happened here. What Mark did to me crowded all those good things – friends, laughter, long walks on campus, downtown, hanging out by the river, parties – right out of my mind."

Her former apartment looked deserted as they drove through the complex, so they went to the manager's office and asked to look inside. The gray-haired lady behind the battered old desk in the office barely glanced up from her novel as she handed them a set of keys. Her dull, uninterested brown eyes returned to her book without so much as a curiosity regarding their intentions. "Knock yourself out."

Muriel picked up the keys and jiggled them in her hand. They could very well be the same set she'd turned in at the same office to a different bored looking gray-haired, browned-eyed lady more than twelve years earlier. They sure looked the same.

Dale stayed slightly behind her as they walked the quarter mile to her former apartment. He stood just close enough she felt his presence as she slipped the key in the lock and turned the knob. As the door opened, she slowly exhaled.

As she stepped inside the bare living room and looked

through to the tiny kitchen, her fear drained away. She walked around the empty living room to the bathroom where she stopped in the middle of a room barely large enough to hold the tub, toilet, and sink. She turned all the way around and looked at Dale. She smiled before she walked out of the bathroom and turned left into the only bedroom in the apartment. She walked around the empty room, paused in front of the single window for a second, and finally sat down in the middle of the room.

She looked up at Dale with a twinkle in her eyes. "It's just an empty apartment. I don't even recognize it anymore. It seems so... I don't know." She paused, turned, and looked out the window. "Empty. Lifeless really." She turned back to him. "It's an erased chalkboard."

Dale smiled and sank down beside her on the floor. She leaned into his arms her back against his chest, and they sat in an embrace while they stared out the window. She squeezed his hands. "Time to go. I'm bored with this place."

A couple of hours later they'd visited four restaurants, two bars, an abandoned building that used to house one of her favorite clothing boutiques, a park by the river, and the grocery store where she'd shopped. "So far this has been easy," she said. "Every place we visit I fear some kind of breakdown, or at least an emotional reaction, because of the connection to Mark. Instead the fear lifts and relief floods over me."

Dale squeezed her hand. "Good." Then searching her eyes. "Right?"

"The tough one is still left. The place where the worst of it happened. Most of these places, though I'd visited them with him, were places where I had to pretend to be normal."

"You weren't the one who wasn't normal."

"No, but at the time I felt anything but normal. I felt

damaged, lost, unworthy."

As they pulled up in front of the place where she'd worked for Mark, Muriel gasped. "I knew he'd moved to a new office building, but I didn't know the old building had been demolished. There's nothing left."

Muriel stepped out of the car and stared at the empty lot between two buildings. A sign at the front of the lot indicated a bookstore and café were scheduled to be built. Dale stood beside her.

She looked up toward the sky and laughed. "I daydreamed about that building's destruction so many times. Of course, in my daydream the building fell right on Mark's head, but I doubt I could get that lucky. Everything has changed. Why did I think it would all be the same? I thought coming back here would be like stepping into my memories."

She walked around the empty lot stopping occasionally to close her eyes. She tried to picture the way things used to be. Her memory didn't hold the detail she always thought it would. She'd thought she could never forget how that office looked, smelled, sounded, and felt. Now she couldn't remember what color - pale green maybe - the walls had been, what the furniture had looked like – some kind of geometric pattern, or what pictures – river scenes or meadows, something outdoorsy - had been on the walls. All this time, she'd thought it was imprinted on her brain, but she couldn't even mentally reconstruct the room when she tried, at least not with certainty.

She turned to Dale and shrugged. "Let's get a cup of coffee. There's a diner just down the street. At least there used to be."

When they returned from the diner an hour later after eating coffee and pecan pie, someone sat on the hood of their rental car and stared into the empty lot. As they came closer, Muriel gasped. "It's Mark. How the hell..."

Dale put his arm around her shoulders. "Maybe it's a coincidence."

"Or maybe someone called him."

"Either way, he's here."

"I'm not ready." She sucked in several quick, shallow breaths.

"Muriel, confronting him is next on your list."

"Yeah, but tomorrow. Tonight was supposed to give me time to prepare. Doing it on my timetable. This feels like relinquishing control like he's stealing control from me." She paused and gasped for breath in several large gulps. "Again."

"Stop." Dale whispered. They stopped suddenly in the middle of the sidewalk. The few people walking down the sidewalk gave them strange looks, shook their heads, and continued on their way.

"Why?"

"Let's take a minute, so you can regain control of the situation."

They stepped into the entrance hall of the closest office building. They sat on the first bench they found. After a few minutes, her breathing calmed, and she looked up. "Okay, I'm ready to deal with this. The sooner I get this over with the sooner I can get on with my life. Maybe for once in his sorry life, Mark's done me a favor though I'm sure that's not his intention."

"There you go." He squeezed her hand. "You can do this. He can't hurt you."

"Right. I can do this."

"I'm right beside you."

"I know." She took a deep breath and slowly exhaled. Her

heartbeat regulated and her breath quieted as she took several slow, deliberate, steady breaths. "I am strong enough. I have the power to handle this. I can do this."

"If you get this over with today, we can relax tomorrow."

"Or do something fun. All this wallowing in the past is getting tiresome." She stood up, squared her shoulders, and smiled. "Let's go."

As they approached the rental car, Mark faced them before he pushed himself off the car with his condescending smirk firmly in place. He looked Muriel up and down in an obvious appraisal of her. She could almost hear the words he's used the first time he appraised her. "You look like a cheap suit in a men's fine clothing shop trying to pass yourself off as something you can never be."

Judgment oozed from him just like then. She stiffened her spine as she waited for his cutting remark. He always expertly landed a verbal punch with the least effort and the maximum impact.

His tailored gray suit and red tie with navy pinstripes lent him an aura of superficial professionalism and power. Muriel understood why people, especially women, believed he possessed both the knowledge and the desire to help them. He'd cultivated an image that hid his depravity behind nice clothes, conservatively cut blonde hair, a welcoming smile, sincere blue eyes, and perfect words. She watched him push his public persona into place as they approached. He probably thought Dale would believe him over anything Muriel said. He believed all men, like him, considered women by their nature, mentally ill.

"Muriel, I heard you were in town. I hope you weren't avoiding me. It's been years." He barely glanced at her as he stepped toward her. He appeared more interested in sizing up Dale than in her.

"Mark, this is my husband, Dale."

"Nice to meet you, Dale." He held out his hand. "What brings you to town?"

"Muriel." Dale ignored Mark's hand and stepped closer to Muriel.

Once Dale's hand touched her lower back in a gesture of support, Muriel looked right into Mark's eyes. "I came here to deal with what you did to me all those years ago. You convinced me I was mentally ill, made me dependent on you for my very life." To her surprise, all the words she'd held inside for so many years poured out in a torrent that sounded like her fantasies but not what she'd practiced. "You used my dependency to control me, manipulate me, and ultimately rape me. You took my shaky self-esteem and destroyed it all in the guise of therapy. There was nothing wrong with me that a little positive interaction and true friendship wouldn't have cured. I was so afraid of you that I went into seclusion. I ran away from here, from you, from the thoughts in my own head. Only I realized I couldn't run away from its effect on me. I had to face the demons you put in my heart and mind. I had to repair the damage you inflicted on my soul and my body. Looking back I can't believe I let a scumbag like you convince me there was something wrong with me. You're the one who needs therapy, you sick fuck." She stopped. Her voice sounded stronger than she expected but her heart felt like it would vibrate right out of her chest while she struggled to inhale deeply enough to fill even half her lungs.

"Guess I can't count on you as a character witness, can I?" He smirked.

She wondered if she imagined the twinkle of joy that appeared in his eyes.

"No, Mark, you can't. What you can count on is I'm going

public with what I know about you. The whole world will know what you've done to me. Everyone will know the kind of man you really are."

He folded his arms. The twinkle disappeared, replaced by icy hardness. "You can't prove anything."

"I won't need to. I'm not the only one you've hurt, or have you forgotten there's already a lawsuit filed against you? Other women will come forward, too. Maybe there'll even be criminal charges."

The smirk disppeared completely. "I've done nothing wrong." His eyes bored into hers.

This time she smiled. "You keep telling yourself that. You're no different than any other rapist."

"You never said no." His tone so cold she expected icicles to form on his lips. "None of you did."

"Just because you convince someone they don't have the right or the ability to say no to you doesn't mean they consent. You use psychology as a weapon just like the common street rapist uses a knife or a gun. What you do may be more despicable, though, because your weapon presents itself as a salvation before you use it to destroy."

"You're a bitch."

"Ouch. Is that the best you can do?" Her tone mocked. She turned to Dale. "Come on, hon, I'm ready to go."

Once they'd driven away, Dale asked. "Do you feel better?"

"For myself, yes. But I meant what I said about going public. He has to be stopped. I realized as soon as I saw him that he won't stop until he's forced to. I'm strong enough to do it now."

"Okay, let's get started. How can I help?"

"Just be there for now. Other than that I don't know yet.

***

Six months later Muriel sat in Ann Morrison Park and stared up at the mountains. As soon as she'd stopped hiding from her past, they'd stopped being symbols and had become just another example of Earth's beauty and diversity. Soon after she went public, more of Mark's victims came forward. The psychiatric board revoked Mark's license to practice psychology.

Criminal charges appeared imminent though much of the evidence was circumstantial and there were issues related to statutes of limitation. The ongoing criminal activity worked against Mark. She regretted not speaking up sooner because her silence allowed him to accumulate victims.

She stretched and smiled at Dale as he walked toward her with a cone of ice cream in each hand. The mountains behind him stood majestic against a beautiful blue sky.

The fortress no longer contained her.

Dumped

Mariella listened to the laughter around her in the hot air balloon as she blinked by the tear in the corner of her blue eyes and pushed her blonde hair into her red hood. As the balloon soared above the earth, she felt more alone than she ever had in her life. Jack broke up with her via email that morning, but she refused to let her money go to waste. So here she stood in a hot air balloon surrounded by couples with love oozing from their pores.

The pilot smiled at her as he began their descent. She smiled back and wondered if he pitied her. She liked his smile and his deep brown eyes. She wondered what color hair his Boise State University Broncos skullcap covered.

She leaned over the edge of the gondola for a better view of their landing. The field where they planned to land appeared to move toward them just as the bottom of the gondola caught on the fence surrounding the field. She leaned farther forward and pointed at the snag just as the pilot shot fire into the balloon. As she slipped over the edge, she mumbled, "Great. Dumped, twice in one day."

It'll Never Happen Again

As dawn approaches, Angel's heart begins to pound. John will soon awaken. She's stared into the darkness for hours contemplating her options. She's terrified of John. His violent outbursts have become more than she can handle. She needs to get away from him. She steels herself against the apologetic lovemaking that always follows his outbursts. Their relationship has become little more than a cliché. The alarm clock sounds.

John rolls over and takes her in his arms, strokes her breast, and mumbles. "Sorry about last night."

"It's okay." She responds quietly. "Me, too." It's the only safe answer she can give.

He kisses her. She fights her nausea as she returns his kiss. He mumbles. "It'll never happen again."

She smiles and avoids looking into his brown eyes. "I know."

He taught her to play the game well.

After their makeup sex, he kisses her as he pushes his curly black hair off his forehead. "All better now. See, I love you."

She nods and replies as expected. "All better now. I know how much you love me. I love you, too. You're the best." It takes all her effort not to gag on the words.

He whistles as he leaves the bed. She attempts to shut out the sound of him singing in the shower as she fights to keep her silent tears from dissolving into uncontrollable sobs. She closes her eyes and pretends to sleep.

A little later she listens to the front door close as he leaves for the office. She slides out of bed and walks into the bathroom. One glance in the mirror reveals she needs to take a sick day. Her right eye is black and blue with a bit of an odd greenish color swirling through it. Her left cheek is still puffy and red. The cut on her lip is covered with crusted blood. She pulls her light brown hair back from her face and secures it with a barrette. She gently washes her face with a cold washcloth.

In the shower, she stands and lets the warm water massage the tension and pain from her shoulders. Tears slip from her brown eyes as she begins to relax. She opens her eyes and studies the fading bruises and healing cuts covering her body. Turning off the shower and wrapping herself in a large navy towel, she replays the previous evening in her mind.

She came home from work and made dinner. John sat down and ate after kissing her lightly on the cheek and grunting at her, as usual. She smiled but only spoke when he asked a question. She knew better than to talk about anything other than what he wanted to discuss.

She can't remember what they argued about, just the painful blows. She winces. It no longer mattered because she finally knew his outbursts were really about control, his need to control her. She's been reading some books at work trying to figure out how to fix the situation. Oh, yeah, last night he became angry when she started the dishwasher and the noise interrupted his television viewing. The previous night he became angered because she didn't start the dishwasher until just before bed. She didn't understand his anger because they couldn't even hear the dishwasher in their bedroom.

She dresses in a pair of old jeans and a faded UK Wildcats sweatshirt. She picks up the phone and calls her work. Once Eli, her boss, answers with his soft hello, she surprises herself by blurting out. "Hi, Eli, it's Angel. I'm sorry to do it like this, but I have to quit."

"Angel, is everything all right?"

She feels tears well in her eyes and can't find the words she wants to say.

"He's been at it again, hasn't he?"

"Yes." Her voice is barely registers a whisper as she hugs herself. She stares out her bedroom window at the parking lot.

"Angel, what are you going to do?"

"I don't know."

"If I can help…"

"Thanks, Eli, but I have to do this on my own." She hangs up the phone.

She fixes herself a bowl of cereal and sits down to watch television. She needs the distraction. She clicks the remote until she finds some talk show discussing spousal murders. Her imagination wanders.

She can't kill him, but she's got to stop this cycle. She can't leave him because he's told her over and over that he won't let her. She knows he's telling the truth because she's tried to leave. He broke her ankle when he caught her.

She doesn't love him anymore, and she's sure he knows it. She fears him though, more than she can find the words to express.

She called the police once, but that hadn't worked out. The officers told her to leave him, especially since they weren't married. He broke her ribs.

How did I get myself into this? What had happened to that sweet, gentle man I fell in love with?

She picks up her purse, pulls out the checkbook, and looks at the balance. Maybe if she runs far enough this time...

But how far is far enough? And what about my parents? He knows where they live. Will he go after them if he can't find me?

She can't go back there. She can't put them in danger. Besides they would drive her crazy finding some way to blame her for John's "temper tantrums" – their words, not hers. She knows better. She stares out the window. She needs to come up with a plan. She can't live like this anymore. She walks through the apartment searching for the answer to fix their life. The apartment offers her nothing but silence and regret hiding in every corner.

She grabs a suitcase from the storage closet and begins to fill it. She has to take the risk. If she does, and he kills her at least this will be over. If she gets away, she can start over. There's no one she will miss, not really anyway. John managed to run off all her friends and even scare most of her family away in the few years they'd lived together. She gets her secret stash of money from her tampon box, the one place he would never look. She counts it even though she already exactly how much she's saved – not nearly enough to start over in a new place. She carries all four suitcases and her purse to her car in two loads.

She drives to the bank. She withdraws half the money from their savings account and half the money from the checking account. She wants to be fair. She doesn't know why, but she does.

She drives toward the local women's shelter. She can't go there. John's best friend's wife works there. She drives around town for the next hour looking for a safe place to make a plan, but she can't find one. John has friends everywhere. She should've made a plan first, but she ran out of time. Hiding money to save for her escape proved more difficult than she expected. She needs to get away from him. Her instincts tell her she needs to go before the damage he inflicts is irreparable. Her inner voice screams at her that to stay is to die.

Her cell phone rings. It's Eli. "Angel, John was just here. He's pissed as hell. Says you and your things are gone from the apartment. I hope that means you've finally left. He was enraged when we told him we didn't know where you were. He didn't believe us. He went nuts in here and broke a bunch of stuff. We've called the police, but I think you'd better ditch your phone and get the hell out of town. Call my wife. She's helped people in these situations before. She'll know what you need to do."

"Thanks, Eli, but I don't want to involve you any more than I already have. I'm sorry. I'll send you some money to cover those damages."

"Don't worry about that. Angel, listen, you'll need help. I've got a sister…."

"Eli, it's okay. I'll drive a good distance out of town, then get on a bus or something. I've got money. Thanks for everything." She hangs up and tosses the phone out the window as she drives over a bridge. She barely hears it splash as it hits the creek.

She drives through the countryside until she reaches the next small town. She pulls into a gas station outside town. She needs gas and some water and food for her trip into the unknown. As she fills the car with gas, she sees a familiar green truck pull in. She watches the tall, muscular form with the buzz haircut and the green eyes step out of the truck and amble toward her. She sees the handgun he's discreetly holding at his side and pointing at her. She doubts anyone else can see it.

Her mind screams for her to move, to get in the car and drive away, but she's glued to the spot, frozen. She wills her body to move, but she can't stop staring at the gun as John walks toward her. Her gaze moves up to meet his. Icy fury and hatred glares from his eyes even though he smiles at her. She jolts into movement.

She calmly pulls the gas nozzle from her car, returns it to the pump, and opens the car door. John grabs her arm. "You're coming with me."

"No, I'm not. Let me go." She pulls away from him, screaming, "It'll never happen again. I won't let it happen again." She runs toward the store.

He fires the gun at her. The bullet brushes her arm as it whizzes by. She runs faster. Another shot rings out just as sirens and flashing lights fill the parking lot of the gas station. She rushes through the door of the store and drops to the floor.

The female clerk, a pretty blonde who looks to be around twenty, grabs her and pulls her behind a shelf filled with candy and potato chips. They watch as John flails the gun around pointing it at one police officer and then another. He turns back toward the store with the gun pointed at the door.

Another shot rings through the air just as the officers shout for him to drop the gun. His bullet breaks the glass in the door of the store. "Sir, put down the gun."

Angel is torn. A part of her wants him to surrender, but

she if he dies he'll never hurt her again. He shoots once more toward the store. "Sir, this is your last chance. Place the gun on the ground and put your hands in the air." The words ring through the air.

John turns with the gun and looks to his right where the voice came from. He drops the gun, falls to his knees and covers his face with his hands. The officers move forward, cuff him, and place him in the back of a patrol car.

Angel rides to the hospital in the back of an ambulance where her flesh wound is treated with a few stitches. A female officer drives her to the women's shelter where John's best friend's wife works, the only one in the county. She calls Eli and lets him know she is safe. "Eli, I'd really like my job back."

"You never quit. You only took a sick day. Right?"

Later that night, Angel sits on her twin bed, little more than a cot really, in the shelter and stares at the wall. Her thoughts continuously replay the last twenty-four hours as tears stream down her cheeks. She hears someone approach her open door and looks up. John's best friend's wife enters. She struggles to remember the woman's name. "Hi, Angel, my name is Mary. How are you tonight?"

"Better than last night." Her smile fails to hide her sadness or her fear.

"Angel, why didn't you ever tell us? We would have helped." Mary pulls over a wooden chair and sits down.

"You're his friends."

"Even so, we would have helped. My father killed my mother during a rage. Friendship or not, I don't tolerate this behavior from anyone. I wished I'd recognized the signs. I can't believe I missed this."

"I was good at hiding it, and he's so charming."

"Still, I'm trained to see these things, but this isn't about me. I just want you to know I'm so sorry I didn't offer you a safe place to reach out for help.

"It's not your fault, Mary."

"It's not yours either, Angel. No matter what he said."

Angel nodded as tears streamed down her cheeks again. "I know. I don't believe it's my fault, but it is my responsibility to change my life now."

"Let's get you settled. Do you need anything? Are you afraid he'll find you?"

"It'll never happen again, Mary."

"That's what they all say."

"Oh, I know. I've heard it often enough. This time I'm saying it. No matter what it takes, it'll never happen again. I won't let it. How do I keep him away from me?"

"We'll work on that."

"Will he go to jail?"

"Probably, but I can't be sure. All I can do is help you find a way to protect yourself from him."

"Okay." She turns toward the wall. "Can we talk about it in the morning? I need some sleep."

"Sure, Angel. I'll come by in the morning. You get some rest. Let us know if you need anything. We're here to help."

She listens to Mary leave the room and sighs. Now she can make a plan. Now she can build a future. Now she can have a life. Now she can feel normal. Now she can... She smiles. For the first time in five long years her future is hers. No one can hold her back now.

She refuses to live in fear any longer even though she doubts John will be cooperative. She's finally strong enough to face whatever the future holds for her. She whispers to herself. "Never again. It'll never happen again."

Soaring

Sheila closed her green eyes and leaned back against Daniel as the hot air balloon lifted off the ground. She tried to fight the cliché, but the thought refused to be quashed "Up, up, and away." She managed to keep the words quiet as she chided herself for such an unoriginal thought. Daniel's arm slipped around her waist, and she looked up into his crystal blue eyes. His lips found hers and lingered a moment. In that instant, she almost forgot about the other people in the gondola.

She smiled at Daniel as her heart swelled with the love she felt for him. She felt so lucky he'd come into her life. He brought peace into her life at a time when she felt the chaos that surrounded her might never end. No matter how hard she pushed him away, he stood his ground but never pushed her for more than she felt ready to give. When she explained to him with a pounding, arguing heart that she couldn't get involved with him, he smiled at her and suggested they just be friends. She heard her words as she agreed to friendship even as she scolded herself for them. When she looked into his eyes, the sincerity she saw won her over. The same sincerity she saw as the balloon soared upward.

Below them she gazed at the winter dormancy of the vineyards of Napa Valley. When Daniel came into her life her heart and soul felt as vacuous as winter fields. Spring promised to bring new life to those fields just as she finally felt ready to let her heart and soul flourish with life again. Perhaps her spring had finally arrived.

As she floated above the vineyards safe in Daniel's arms, she finally felt ready to remember without fear. She travelled a long voyage to her current life, but she felt grateful she survived it. Her heart pounded at the thought. Far too many times she had wished she hadn't survived the ordeal to be forced to deal with the aftermath it wreaked on her life.

She looked out at the gray sky and hoped rain wouldn't interrupt their plans to tour vineyards and wineries before they ended the day with a nice long walk around the town of Sonoma.

Rain! It rained that day, too; poured to be exact. She closed her eyes and tried to stop the shiver that spread though her body like electricity through a live wire. "Cold, honey?" Daniel whispered in her ear.

"A little." She smiled and hoped he wouldn't read the truth in her eyes.

He held her gaze. "It's not going to rain today."

"Doesn't matter if it does. We'll have fun as long as we're together."

His arms tightened. "I know the rain brings up those memories."

"So we'll make new memories. Happy memories." She kept her voice determined. She pushed her long dark hair behind her ear and exhaled.

Sheila slipped her hands inside her navy blue peacoat to

warm them and shivered again as she felt the scar that ran from her left hip to her left breast through her pink silk shirt. She'd always carry that reminder with her. There was no way to escape it. Not that she could forget anyway. The scars on her heart and soul remained just as prominent even if invisible to the naked eye.

She slipped her fingers away from the scar and turned her attention to the pilot's spiel. "That's Domaine Chandon below us."

She looked down as Daniel whispered. "Is that one on our list?"

"Yes."

"Good. Looks like there's an outdoor patio. I hope it's not too cold to sit out there and sip a glass of wine."

"Umm. Sounds nice."

She closed her eyes and snuggled back into him. The words to express how good it felt to feel so safe escaped her. Life stripped safety from her so long ago. She appreciated her sense of security much more than before she'd felt so lost, abandoned, and forgotten. Daniel hadn't saved her. The space he gave her to vanquish the ghosts lingering in her heart and mind allowed her to save herself.

Sheila shivered as cold wind touched her face just before the pilot pulled the lever that fired the balloon and sent them higher while it dispersed a sudden rush of fleeting warmth. She looked around at the other people in the balloon. She and Daniel shared a section of the gondola with a couple who chatted and snapped photos without pause. Behind them, in the adjacent, section, two couples talked nonstop. She heard the chatter of conversations on the other side of the balloon but couldn't differentiate between the words well enough to understand the context.

Suddenly, the chatter enveloped her. Her breath caught in

her throat. She felt transported back to that room again where she heard the voices but she couldn't make a sound to get their attention to help her because he'd choked her until she barely managed to force out a whimper.

"Sheila! Honey! Sheila! Breathe. Come on. Breathe. Sheila."

She shivered, snapped out of her memory and took a deep breath. She reached back and pulled Daniel closer to her. "I'm okay. Just a memory."

"I'm sorry."

"It's not your fault. There's no reason such a beautiful experience should bring up those memories. It's my own problem. I need to learn how to enjoy the moment and let go of the past."

"Don't be so hard on yourself, babe. You're doing great. Remember, Dr. Ellers said you have to be patient with yourself."

"I know. I know." She smiled up at him. "Just look at the sky. It's so beautiful."

"The clouds are drifting away."

"I wish my past would drift away with them."

He pulled her into a bear hug from behind and kissed the top of her head. She reached up and rubbed her hand against the navy blue skull cap covering his short, dark brown hair. She sighed. She never thought she'd find this kind of tenderness. She believed herself too damaged to deserve it for far too long.

Daniel hated it when she referred to herself as damaged goods. The thought invaded her soul and set up shop in her heart a long time ago. Such a total invasion of her body left her with little to convince herself of her worth or that she deserved anyone or anything good in her life.

She allowed Marshall to steal so much from her. True, she

couldn't control his behavior, but a part of her believed she should've foreseen what he planned. Somehow she should've read his mind. Somehow she should've protected herself. Somehow she should've stopped him. Somehow she should have....

She wished she felt comforted by the knowledge he fooled other people at well. All her friends adored him. She considered him her best friend for over a year before things changed.

She never considered him anything more than a friend. She never considered that when she casually changed in front of him or talked about her sex life that he even noticed. He never reacted – at least not visibly. She always thought of him as an interested friend who provided her with a different perspective on life.

The hugs, the evenings cuddling in front of the television, the long heart-to-heart talks had all seemed like contact with a caring brother who always understood her. Little did she know the effect all this had on him until it was too late. Since she felt no attraction to him and was so sure he was attracted to men, she never considered the possibility he felt attracted to, much less obsessed with, her.

Sheila felt the balloon beneath her shift. It couldn't be time for them to land yet. The pilot pulled the lever sending a flame up into the balloon. They rose higher. She leaned forward to look over the edge of the gondola. Daniel's hands tightened on her waist. She smiled reveling in the safety she felt whenever she was near him. That security came from his intense loyalty, caring heart, giving nature, and gentle soul. It had taken her a long time to trust her judgment when she recognized these qualities in him. She'd thought she saw the same qualities in Marshall until he proved her wrong.

Marshall invited her over for dinner and a movie. Shortly

after dinner, she'd felt drowsy. She fought to keep her eyes open while they watched a thriller. The next thing she remembered she awoke when she tried to scratch her nose and discovered both hands restrained. She opened her eyes and saw photos of herself, notes she'd written, and several items she'd been trying to find for several months including a hairbrush, a lipstick, a porcelain doll her grandmother gave her years earlier, and a pair of her panties displayed on the wall she faced. She attempted to pull her hands free even though she could feel the metal of the handcuffs and knew her attempts were futile.

"Now, now, Sheila, calm down. Everything will be okay." Marshall stepped into the room carrying a quilt. When he spread it out, she recognized the double wedding ring pattern. "Beautiful, isn't it? My grandma made it. You're the first person to use it."

"Marshall, what are you doing?" She struggled to keep her voice calm.

"Making sure you're warm enough."

"No, Marshall, I mean why do you have me handcuffed to the bed?"

"Because you need to see that I can make you enjoy being involved with someone again." He ran his hand through his curly, dark blond hair.

"Someone?"

"Well, me."

"Forced?"

"Well, you are resistant to giving love another chance."

"Marshall." She steadied her voice and hoped she could somehow convince him to let her go. *After all he was a good guy at heart, wasn't he?* "I told you I'm taking a break from dating to get my priorities straight, so I'll make better decisions for myself and my future."

"No, you're avoiding getting close to people. You're avoiding intimacy." He adjusted the covers around her. "There. You'll see. I'm right about this."

"Marshall, this" She shook her handcuffed hands. "isn't necessary."

He smiled for a moment before panic crossed his brown eyes. "Damn, I forgot. You must be starving. It's been a long time since you ate. I'll be right back with your lunch. You slept right through breakfast." He left the room.

She fell back against the pillows he'd stacked on the bed. She needed a plan. She struggled to reconcile her situation with the Marshall she knew. It made no sense. This man she thought she knew so well turned out to be a complete stranger.

Over the next couple of days he bathed her, fed her, dressed her, and kept her tucked into bed. He even exercised her legs like she remembered the nurses doing for her bedridden grandmother several years earlier. He did all of it with a gentleness that confused her. She tried to figure out his intentions. She expected him to rape her and felt relieved every time he left the room without showing in interest in violating her sexually.

On the third day, he left the apartment. As soon as she heard his car start, she started to scream for help. He lived on a busy street, and she heard people outside. She screamed until she her voice turn hoarse and her throat felt raw, but no on came to her aid.

Marshall shook his head as he entered the room. "Now why would you scream? Haven't I taken good care of you? I've not hurt you. I'm giving you everything you need."

"Let me go." Her voice squeaked as she struggled to get the words out. "You're holding me *prisoner*."

"I'm taking care of you." His eyes expressed no

compassion.

"I want to go home."

"You are home. Accept that."

"No, I want to be free."

"Why can't you just be happy?"

"Because you have me handcuffed to a bed. Because you've cut me off from everyone I know. Because you're holding me prisoner."

She felt cold metal slide up her side a moment before she felt the searing pain of her skin parting. Marshall smiled at her. "Sheila, love, no more screaming." His voice sounded soft and loving. She wanted to vomit. He tucked a couple of towels under her side and left the room whistling.

Blood escaped from the wound and trickled across her skin. She panicked. She feared she might bleed to death. Unable to see the wound or touch it with her hand she could only imagine its depth and severity.

Sheila's panic increased when she started to feel sleepy. She struggled to keep her eyes open. She refused to fall asleep. She refused to die. Her thoughts tumbled as she tried to make sense of his behavior. *Is he trying to kill me? What happened to the sweet guy who has been my friend though a horrendous breakup and a multitude of failed attempts to start new relationships? What did he think all those times I cried on his shoulder? Did he somehow mistake my trust in him, my affection for him as somehow romantic? Did I do something to lead him on? How can I get out of this situation? How can I survive?*

Marshall woke her as he applied alcohol to her side. She recognized the smell as well as the burning sensation. He gently placed a bandage over the wound and taped it to her skin. He tenderly turned her face toward his and smiled. His voice somehow managed to take on both soothing and menacing notes as he spoke. "No more screaming. Okay? I don't like disciplining you. It hurts me."

"Hurts you?" She managed before he put a finger in front of her mouth and shook his head.

"You ruined tonight. I had special plans for us. Now you'll just have to wait for your surprise." His voice actually sounded sad as he rolled a white silk handkerchief into a rope-like shape, forced it into her mouth, and tied it behind her head. Then he picked up his tray of first aid supplies and left the room.

The next evening Marshall walked into the room carrying a garment bag. He bathed her before he dressed her in an expensive-looking red evening gown with matching stilettos and changed the handkerchief in her mouth to a red one that matched the dress. He fixed her hair and put makeup on her face. He didn't speak a word as he prepared her. When he finished, he left the room without speaking.

A few minutes later Marshall returned to the room pushing a wheeled table set for a romantic dinner complete with roses and candles. He released one handcuff from the bed and pulled her toward the side of the bed as far as the other handcuff would allow. He attached the handcuff to a chair beside the bed. Then he did the same with the other handcuff making sure to never free her hands. He pushed the chair across the room to a bathroom. He lifted her dress over the back of the seat and pulled her panties down. He pushed chair over the toilet and pulled out enough of the seat to allow her to use the toilet. It was the first time since she'd awoken that he hadn't forced her to use a bedpan. He closed the bathroom door, and she quickly glanced around hoping for a means of escape. She saw only one door and no window. Her heart pounded because she saw no options.

After several minutes, he returned, cleaned her, and arranged her clothes back in place.

As he pushed her back into the bedroom, she panicked. He'd changed the bed and covered it with red rose petals leaving no doubt about his intentions for the evening. The intentions she most feared. A sea of white candles lit the room. He pushed her chair up to the table and stepped behind her. When he pulled a chair next to hers, she saw he wore a tuxedo. He laid a white rose, her favorite, on her lap and smiled at her. "For the lady."

He removed the handkerchief from her mouth and kissed her lips. He fed her and himself salad, lobster, bread, and champagne. He served strawberries dipped in chocolate for dessert. A bite for her, then a bite for him until he decided dinner ended. Then he kissed her again and moved her back onto the bed reversing his earlier process. He uncuffed each hand from the chair then cuffed it to the bed. Her heart pounded. Her body shook. Panic claimed her. "Marshall?"

"Sshh. You need to be quiet."

"Do you have…"

"Do you want the handkerchief back?"

She shook her head.

"Then you must be quiet. Otherwise I'll assume you like the handkerchief."

"Please don't."

He put his finger to her lips. "Last chance. Do you understand?"

She nodded.

He slowly undressed her. He kissed her bare skin as he peeled the clothes away. She felt tears well up in her eyes as she struggled to keep quiet. When he pulled off her panties, her fear overcame her. A sob slipped out. He appeared not to notice. He stood and removed his clothes.

She closed her eyes and focused on the sound of the falling rain as she fought back the impulse to scream though she had no voice left to scream. Terror of his reaction silenced even an attempt to scream. She turned her head to the side. Tears streamed down her cheeks as he forced himself inside her. She felt him lean over her and force the handkerchief back into her mouth and tie it behind her head again. "I think you like the handkerchief. It's the only way you'll keep quiet." He whispered against her ear before he kissed it. She hadn't even realized she'd made a sound.

When he finished, he slapped her face. She opened her eyes as he began to beat her body randomly. "Damn, Sheila, I looked forward to our first time for so long and you just lay there the whole time. And what the hell is with those tears? What a fucking disappointment you turned out to be. You're really not worth all the trouble I've gone to. You could've shown a little enthusiasm at least. I made it a special evening and you ruined everything. What a fuckin' waste. I'm outta here." He grabbed his clothes and stalked out of the room. He left her naked, bleeding, beaten and battered still handcuffed to the bed with her mouth gagged. A few minutes later she heard the front door slam, and she started vigorously chewing on the handkerchief.

Before long she started to drift off to sleep despite her efforts to fight the drowsiness. Marshall must have drugged her again.

She awoke as paramedics loaded her into an ambulance. She later learned the police received an anonymous call that led them to rescue her. The police never found Marshall, and she never heard from him again.

Daniel's light kiss on her neck brought her out of her flashback. She sighed.

Life put her in a hot air balloon over Napa Valley with Daniel, the man who provided her exactly the kind of support she needed to regain her life, reliving the ordeal once again. She sighed. *Will I get past this? Will it ruin every beautiful moment in my life?*

She looked up into Daniel's face. This man offered her so much. She refused to allow her past to ruin that. She silently vowed with intensified resolve to move on with her life, to not let Marshall win by invading and destroying every good thing in her life, and to give her all to creating the future she wanted with Daniel.

She opened her arms wide reaching out of the gondola symbolically releasing all the pain and fear still trapped in her heart. She let out a long breath and felt Daniel's presence as he gently placed his hands on her hips and stepped back from her. Somehow he seemed to sense she needed to stand on her own for this release. She pulled in a deep breath, closed her eyes, and turned. She tiptoed, threw her arms around his neck, hugged him, pulled back and looked into his eyes. She felt freer than she had in years. She looked out over Napa Valley and smiled. No matter what came before or what came next, in this moment she soared above the world on a cloud of happiness.

Coming Soon

Red (A Novel)

Chapter 1

Tears streamed down Marissa's cheeks, her long light brown hair fell over her face and stuck to her cheeks. Marissa sat in the middle of her kitchen surrounded by those she loved – the only three people in the world who mattered to her. She stared at them, clueless as to what she should do next.

The sun streaking the sky with oranges, pinks, and purples interrupted by gray rolling clouds, the wind blowing through the trees in the backyard, and the distant sounds of thunder signaling an approaching storm felt like a different reality. One in which she had no place. The evening storm moved toward the house, finally cooling the sun's rays which had punished anyone who dared step outdoors all day. She barely heard the thunder crash – louder, closer. The red in front of her blocked out everything else as it consumed her.

She ran her index finder through the sea of red covering the white ceramic tile floor. Her eyes refused to look up. If she didn't see the source of the red maybe, just maybe, she could convince herself it was only paint. Paint. Yeah, that was it. Paint. Red paint. Lots of red paint. She whispered the word aloud, or did she? "Paint."

It didn't surround those she loved so dearly. It couldn't. They didn't deserve the red. The flood of red came after her like it had so many times before. *Why wouldn't it stop?*

Her ivory pants darkened as the red spread over them. She watched it but couldn't force herself to move away from the sensation of wetness against her knees. She should move. She needed to call for help, but she couldn't move, couldn't speak, couldn't breathe. Her mind froze and her body paralyzed in place.

Her loved ones came into focus as she lifted her head. They lay next to each other on the floor. The red oozed from their bodies blending with the red surrounding her. She shook her head. Streaks of blood created paths from her to them. She looked to her side and picked up the bloodstained 8-inch serrated bread knife. She would join her family. Yes, that's what she'd do. It was the only answer. Two bloody bread crumbs dropped from the knife and landed on her upper thigh. She leaned forward. She felt the red dye her ivory camisole and her forehead. Red never stayed where it belonged. Her hand wound around the blade. The cold, hard steel cut through the skin on her palm, but she felt little more than a tingling sensation. She closed her eyes. The fight left her. The red could have her.

The tip of the knife cut through her paints and separated the skin on her leg. She continued the slow, precise movement without so much as a change of expression. Blood seeped from the wound in her leg and the gash in her hand.

A sudden, large crash of thunder and a flash of lightning interrupted the ominous quiet. The rain had yet to come. Marissa shuddered still focused on the encroaching red. This time her defenses were gone. It would take her like it had threatened so many times before.

Minutes passed.

She sat up and stared at the motionless bodies spread in a

neat row in the entrance from the family room to the kitchen. The knife dropped from her hand with a clang as metal hit ceramic. She twitched her nose against the assault of a coppery odor. Her gaze traveled from one lifeless body to the next. From the small, pretty girl to the even smaller cute boy to the handsome man. They shared enough features to prove they were related. *Who were these people? Why am I sitting in this room with them? Where am I? Do they mean something to me? Should they mean something to me? How did they get here? How did I get here?*

Marissa turned her head toward a rustling noise in the backyard. Her green eyes met the red-rimmed, tear filled, green eyes of a stranger in her reflection in the sliding glass doors. She shuddered as the thought of evil lurking nearby washed over her. She pushed her hair away from her face. The door stood slightly open and the wind whipped through the space, whistling a barely audible whine. Or was that sound stuck in her throat trying to get out?

Well-known sounds in the next room attracted her attention. She looked around to find the source of the sounds. Tom chased Jerry on the television. Between her and the television lay those familiar, lifeless bodies surrounded by a sea of rising red. Her body shook violently as she struggled to bring the bodies into face, to remember what she needed to remember, to understand what stood just beyond her comprehension.

She clutched her head in her hands. *Who the hell were these people?* She needed to remember. She knew they were important. It was important she remember them. She pulled her hair *How did the red find them? How had they gotten here? What had happened to them?* She beat her bloody hands against her blood-covered face. Thoughts, so many thoughts, kept swirling in her head. They made no sense. Faces and red and people and red and places and red. Always the red. She couldn't stop the red. Too much red.

Rain beat against the sliding glass door and the kitchen window matching the banging inside her head. Marissa continued to beat her hands against her face but otherwise remained still.

She heard sirens in the distance. Help was on the way....

Red is schedule for release in 2015!

Vulnerability in Silhouette: Poems

Vulnerability's reputation often causes it to be maligned. Vulnerability creates insecurity and destroys confidence. Delve into the human experience of balancing vulnerability and strength while finding one's place in the world. Explore the strength in vulnerability and the vulnerability in strength through soul-searching poems that travel the full spectrum of vulnerability from weakness to silhouette.

Vulnerability in Silhouette is scheduled for release in 2015!

Book List

Fiction

All She Ever Wanted

When Victoria, who is white, meets Daryn, who is African American, she has no idea the effect he and his family will have on her life. As she struggles for the success she's certain will make her parents proud, Daryn's family introduces her to a new definition of love, family, acceptance, and success. Victoria and Daryn struggle to keep their friendship intact as they are faced with the prejudices of family, friends, and lovers. The empty place in Victoria's heart forces her to face all she's sacrificed in her quest for success including friendship, love, family, and grief.

Poetry

Love in Silhouette: Poems

Love. We long for it. We feel the sting of love's loss. We give love in hopes of receiving love. We withhold love out of fear it won't be returned. Love connects us. Love disappoints us. Love distinguishes us. Love extinguishes us. Love abandons us. Love creates expectations. Love fulfills lives. Love is always a risk worth exploring even when it fails. Love is poetry... Poetry is love... Love becomes a silhouette.

Reflections in Silhouette: Poems

The journey for the truth of self offers the opportunity for triumph and failure. Often as we search for who we're meant to be in life, we misplace ourselves for a little while. Even when we're struggling to reconnect with our misplaced cores, we can't help but be ourselves. Life is simply a journey to fill in the gaps, to find our truths, to become our best selves. When we embrace the all of who we are, we live richer, fuller lives and avoid being simply reflections in silhouette...

Memory in Silhouette: Poems

Every moment is a memory and every memory is a moment. Memories are moments that build on one another to create the foundation of who we are at any given point in life. Memories - good, bad, and neutral - meld within our minds and hearts housing love, hate, pleasure, fear, anger, and happiness. With each memory we make, we become more compassionate, and therefore more connected to the world around us. Our strengths and weaknesses live in our memories creating the complexity and simplicity that encompasses the full human experience. Come along to discover how moments blossom into growth or become merely a memory in silhouette...

Strength in Silhouette: Poems

We revere strength. We malign strength. We both fear and admire strength. When we reach inside during our weakest moments and find the strength to move forward, we discover the best thing about being human. Our humanity lies in both the strengths and the weaknesses that connect us and separate us. The poems within explore the many facets of strength in the hopes we never allow strength to become merely a silhouette.

Praise for T. L. Cooper's books

Strength in Silhouette

"...Often harsh in its realism, it also can soar with delicate and unexpected nuance..." - Lucy

Memory in Silhouette

"...pithy examination of relational memories should help every poet discover an inner part of their own memories. I highly recommend this poetic study in life lived and memories examined." – Auburn McCanta, author of All the Dancing Birds

Reflections in Silhouette

"...Brave enough to lower the curtain into her own heart, T.L. gives the reader that certain leverage where one might be able to find the strength, upon reflection, to go forward into the bright sunshine of their own new day..." - Ray Ellis, author of the Nate Richards Series.

Love in Silhouette

"...Love in Silhouette" is a delightfully honest and open-faced collection of poetry that leaves you feeling as though you have peeked in on intimate moments of the author's love life..." - Mary Braun, co-author of Opposites Attract: A Haiku Tete-a-Tete.

All She Ever Wanted

"...A thoughtful, insightful look into the changing human mind and spirit evoked by an interracial friendship, All She Ever Wanted is a superbly written, highly recommended novel showcasing a theme that is as historic and universal as interracial human experience, and contemporary as today's newspaper headlines..." - Midwest Book Review.

About the Author

T. L. Cooper is an author and poet. Her poems, short stories, articles, and essays have appeared online, in books, and in magazines. Her published books include a novel, All She Ever Wanted, and her Silhouette Poetry Series. She grew up on a farm in Tollesboro, Kentucky. She studied corrections and psychology at Eastern Kentucky University. When not writing, she enjoys yoga, golf, and traveling.